MW01134518

DEADLY NIGHT, SILENT NIGHT

Strong Women, Extraordinary Situations
Book Eight

Margaret Daley

Copyright

Deadly Night, Silent Night
Copyright © 2016 by Margaret Daley

Strong Women, Extraordinary Situations Series

Deadly Hunt, Book 1

Deadly Intent, Book 2

Deadly Holiday, Book 3

Deadly Countdown, Book 4

Deadly Noel, Book 5

Deadly Dose, Book 6

Deadly Legacy, Book 7

Deadly Night, Silent Night, Book 8

ONE

As Rebecca Howard's meeting with the key personnel at Outdoor Sports and Recreation came to an end, she finally relaxed back in her chair at the conference table. "This is the twenty-fifth anniversary of the company and our Christmas holiday season. With the addition of the Port Bering's store last month, we have eight in the state. Now it's time to expand to the rest of the states. I'll make the announcement at OSR's grand celebration the first week in December."

She scanned each face of the five members of her executive committee, coming to rest on Clint. When she looked at her twin brother, she saw a younger version of her father and hoped she was fulfilling her dad's dream for the business he'd started with one small store. She wished both of her parents were here to see how big his vision had become. Their deaths still brought sadness. Too many important people in her life had died.

"Rebecca?"

She blinked and focused on Clint. "Sorry. Thinking about that first store." She'd been eleven when it had opened. Forcing a smile, she turned her attention to the group. "I'll need your final reports on your part of the celebration on my desk by five o'clock tomorrow. I don't want anything to go wrong." She rose as her team left.

Except for Clint. "When this is over, are you going to take that vacation you keep putting off?"

"What if I don't?" She gathered the pad she'd jotted down notes on and skirted her big oak desk to settle in the chair behind it.

"I'll sic Tory and Laura on you."

She pictured her best friends ganging

up on her and laughed. "They haven't been able to change me yet. Let's face it. I love my work. This is where I belong." And she really felt that except when she saw Tory, Clint's wife, with their nine-month old baby. Family had always been important to Rebecca. She'd wanted children with her husband, but he'd died before she became pregnant. She'd replaced the emptiness she'd felt with work.

"That's what our dad would have said."

Her brother was right, but she wasn't going to say that out loud. "Don't you have to drive to Fairbanks today?"

Clint made his way to the door. "Dismissing me won't stop my worrying, Rebecca. I'm going to pester you like you did me when I came back to Alaska. I know what overload and burnout can do to a person."

When her twin disappeared, she stared at the door he'd shut, unable to shake the fact she'd almost lost her brother, too, not because he was a captive in a war zone but from a mad man who'd meant to kill Tory. Rebecca had a lot of acquaintances but few

3

people she trusted—Clint and Tory were two of them.

She shook her head. Why was she thinking about the past so much today?

If she'd realized the anniversary would cause her to remember the past at odd times, she wouldn't have come up with the celebration. She shoved the memories into a box and slammed the lid closed.

Shifting toward her computer, she opened her e-mails and began working her way through them. But ten minutes later, her screen went blank. She restarted it. Nothing. Oh, great. Something was wrong with her desktop. This would be the second time in a week tech support would have to come fix it. This computer was only a year old, but maybe she needed a new one.

She reached to call Neil Sanders, the head of the tech support, but before she could pick up the receiver, a rap on her door sounded, followed by her landline ringing as well as her cell phone. She started to answer the one on her desk when her administrative assistant barged into the office, her usual unruffled façade gone.

Rebecca let the calls go to voicemail. "What's wrong?"

"The computers are down throughout the building," Susan Maxwell said, planting herself in front of Rebecca's desk.

"In the store, too?"

Her administrative assistant nodded. "Neil called and asked for you to come downstairs."

Used to things going wrong, Rebecca pushed to her feet and started for the elevator. Hopefully, it was something minor that could be repaired quickly. The doors swished open, and she stepped on. Alone, she punched the button for the first floor then leaned back against the wall. She thrived on challenges, but this was the third problem that had come out of left field within the past two weeks. First, someone set off a stink bomb in the main store, and the security camera didn't catch any useful information. Then late yesterday, OSR in Fairbanks was robbed.

Passing the second floor, she straightened, preparing to—the elevator stopped and the lights went off. For a few seconds, panic descended. The sense of feeling trapped threatened her composure. She struggled to drag air into her lungs while she fumbled for the cell phone in her jacket pocket.

Its bright light illuminated the small area of the elevator, and she noticed Clint had called her about the time she'd been talking to Susan. Rebecca tapped the screen to return it. No connection. That was ridiculous. She always had cell reception in the store. Could that go down with the computers and power? It shouldn't. This place had never been a dead zone. What was going on?

When the emergency lights flickered on, she breathed a little easier that the backup generator had kicked in. She paced the elevator, trying to find a spot where she could use her cell. After covering the whole area, she decided there wasn't one.

First, she tried the elevator buttons, pushing all of them. Nothing. Then she searched for a way out. She couldn't reach the hatch in the top of the elevator. This was when being five feet three inches was a disadvantage. That left the door.

Sweat dampened her palms and forehead as her heart thumped against her rib cage. The sensations reminded her of the time she had been trapped in an abandoned refrigerator when playing hide and seek with her brother and friends. The more she yelled and used up her oxygen the harder it had been to breathe.

Her pulse rate accelerated, and she stuffed her phone in her pocket while she tried to pry the doors apart. She couldn't.

She again punched the buttons for the four floors, but she didn't go up or down. She hit the alarm bell. In the elevator next to her, someone screamed and struck the doors. Another person tried to quiet the woman, but she only grew louder.

Rebecca paced, the screams from the elevator next to hers fueling her own panic.

Stay calm. There are a lot of people in the building. They know the elevators are stalled because of the power outage. Help will arrive soon.

* * *

Detective Alex Kincaid exited his SUV and headed for Outdoor Sports and Recreation's main store. A childhood friend, Clint Howard, came out of the double glass doors and met him in the parking lot.

"Glad you could come." Clint shook Alex's hand. "I know you usually don't handle stuff like this, but I don't have a good feeling. We've had a couple of other incidents within the last two weeks involving this store and the one in Fairbanks. I hope this isn't a pattern forming."

"What went wrong?"

Clint told him about a robbery in Fairbanks and a stink bomb in their main store.

The stink bomb could be a prank, but an armed robbery in Fairbanks definitely wasn't. Alex hadn't heard that at the station yet. "What's happened today? Anything besides, the computers going down and the power off?"

"I've directed our employees to

facilitate taking care of our customers as much as possible and directing them to the exits. I understand something's caused all the computers and anything they control to shut down, but that occurred several minutes before the power went out."

"So the power outage didn't cause the computer system to go down."

"No. Neil thinks it could be a virus, but we won't know until later." As customers streamed out of the store, Clint rubbed his nape, watching the flood of people leaving. "I had our security guard check the breakers for the power, and they're fine. Now they're searching for what caused the outage. Our backup generator is powering some lights and other essential areas, one being the PA system. Initially, in the few seconds the power was out, confusion occurred. I was at the front and quickly made an announcement, explaining what happened, which seemed to calm the people in the store."

"If the breakers aren't the cause, then something more serious is happening. The transformer?"

"George Baker, head of security, is checking on it out back."

"What about the computers? That happened first. Are they working since the emergency power came on?" Alex held a door open, and Clint entered first.

"No. We're focusing on rescuing the people trapped in three of our four elevators. The emergency generator powers the one that's still working. And if the computer problems had been caused by the power outage, part of that system would be back up as well."

"This, after a stink bomb set off recently. Definitely something more is going on here." His jaw clenched, Alex scanned the dimly lit store. "Is Rebecca here?"

"Her assistant told me she was on her way downstairs. I've tried to call her on my cell phone. It wouldn't work. I've never had problems using it here in the store. Thankfully, our landlines are operational."

"So do you think Rebecca's stuck in the elevator?" Clint had been with Alex when he found her in an old refrigerator during a game of hide and seek. She'd almost suffocated. If they had opened the door five minutes later, she would have been dead. From that day forward, he'd watched over her—from a distance. He'd been working himself up to ask her out when they were sophomores in high school, but before he did, she gave her heart to Cade Tucker who later married her after graduation. It had been for the best. Alex was dedicated to his job.

"Probably, since she was coming down to see Neil. I have a couple of employees trying to keep the passengers calm until the fire department arrives. They should be here any minute."

"And you're worried." It wasn't a question. Alex had known Clint since childhood, and when he was most concerned, he shut down emotionally and went on autopilot. They were similar in their reactions.

"She wouldn't ride the elevator for years. It's only been the last few that she braved it. She figured if I could get over my fear to save Tory then she could overcome hers. You know how competitive she can be."

Alex chuckled. "Yes. She can outshoot me."

A security guard rushed up, breathing hard. "The transformer is down. Sparks are flying. The firefighters just arrived. They're seeing to that."

The fire department would have been called to rescue whoever was in the elevators. At least they would be on the scene to deal with the transformer. "Make sure people stay away in case it explodes." Alex turned to Clint. "I'm calling in additional help. We need to empty the building except for essential personnel. Something is going on here. I don't think all this would happen by accident."

"George, we'll take care of the elevators while the firefighters are busy with the transformer. Send as many of the emergency team that you can spare to find tools to help open the doors." When the head of security left, Clint continued, "Rebecca formed a group of employees to respond to any kind of emergency, manmade or natural, to protect our customers and employees. George heads it as well as our security."

"I'm calling the station." Alex took out his cell phone then remembered the reception was down.

"You can use our landline in the manager's office. That's the nearest one."

As Alex followed Clint to an office at the front of the building, he tried his cell anyway, but no bars appeared. The uneasy feeling in the pit of his stomach grew.

* * *

Someone shouted through the doors that help was on the way. Chewing on her nails, Rebecca prowled the car, which was growing smaller the longer she stayed trapped in it. She had to control her rising panic. She couldn't function if she let it take over. Glancing at her watch, she calculated she'd been in the elevator twenty minutes. She checked her cell phone, but it was still useless. The urge to bang on the doors threatened her. All she would end up doing was hurting her hands and scaring the people in the other ones.

This is not the refrigerator. I'm all right. God is with me.

She concentrated on the sounds coming from the other side of the doors, but the staccato of her heartbeat thumped against her eardrums, drowning them out. When the elevator doors began to open slowly a few minutes later, she sagged against the wall, clasping her trembling hands and relishing the rush of fresh air into the car. She wouldn't have suffocated, but she couldn't shake her childhood memories of being confined in a space she could hardly move in, let alone breathe.

Stuck between the second and first floor, she knelt by the three-foot gap. The first face she spied was Alex Kincaid. His smile chased away the fear she'd fought for the past twenty-five minutes. When his gray gaze connected with hers, all remnants of anxiety and panic fled.

She gave him a grin. "It's about time you came."

"Clint said you'd say something like

that. He's working on another elevator."

Alex. He'd been the one who opened the refrigerator door and rescued her from near death. Her smile faded.

"Rebecca?"

Alex's deep voice whisked her back to the present, and she stared at his familiar face, comforted by it.

"You okay?"

"Of course. I knew it wouldn't be long before I got out." She sat on the floor and wiggled forward until her legs dangled. "I hope you're going to catch me."

"When have I let you down?" Alex took hold of her ankles.

"How about that time I fell into the river and nearly froze to death?"

"I threw you a rope."

Which she'd barely caught before the current dragged her away. "Okay. That was probably the best thing for you to do." They had only been twelve and had gotten lost from the rest of the hikers, but Alex had kept his cool and gotten her out, soaked but alive. "That was the second time I owed you my life."

She scooched forward, slipping out of the car and into Alex's arms, reminding her of when he'd pulled her from the water and immediately slung his dry coat around her shoulders. She peered up into his glimmering eyes, the color of the river—like sunlight glinting off pewter—that day.

They turned dark. The angular lines of his face set in a serious expression. "Are you really all right?"

Still plastered against his tall, muscular frame, she felt the cage of his arms and realized she needed to step away. She glanced to the side; a few employees were watching. Putting some distance between them, she replied, "Yes. I'm fine. Not much gets me down." Rebecca lifted her chin a notch, her look challenging him to disagree.

Her brother helped an older woman out, the ashen cast to her skin and her trembling indicating she had been the person who'd lost control. Clint would know what to do.

Behind her, Alex leaned forward and whispered into her ear, "It's okay to admit you aren't."

"I am."

He reached around and lifted her left hand. "You always bite your nails when you're nervous and upset."

She tugged her arm away. Her father had thought that was a sign of weakness, and she'd tried to break the habit, but every once and a while it crept back. "Okay. I may have had a little problem, but as you can see, I'm fine now. That's all that counts."

While the area around the elevators was clearing and Clint escorted the frightened lady toward the front of the store, Rebecca swung around, making sure no one was close to overhear her. "What happened? Do you know anything?"

"Not much. The transformer's down. That's why the power went off. Nothing definite about why your computer system shut down. I've called in more uniforms and the K-9 unit to search the building. And now that the people are out of the elevators, we need to evacuate the store until my men have checked it. We're the last to leave." Alex started for the back door nearby.

Rebecca lengthened her strides to keep up with him. "What do you believe it is? You think there's a bomb in here." She wouldn't forget the serial bombing last year and the havoc the bomber had caused in Anchorage.

Alex held the door open for her. "Probably not but these two incidents happening together indicate it was coordinated."

"I'm glad to see I'm not paranoid. That's what I think, too."

"We'll know when the causes for the power outage and computer shutdown are discovered."

Rebecca made her way in the direction of the transformer and a group of firefighters. A burning stench infused the air, growing stronger the closer she came to the captain of the fire department, who was talking to someone from the electric company.

She approached them as dark smoke poured out of the transformer, but no flames. "Is it safe now?"

"No," the captain said, glancing at Alex as he joined them. "I need the whole area roped off. These kinds of fires are dangerous and unpredictable. I'll let you know when it's safe."

"I'll put some men on it." Alex placed his hand on the small of Rebecca's back.

Reluctantly, she walked with him to the side of the building. She'd hoped the smoke meant the fire was burning out. But as she rounded the corner, she slowed down and peered over her shoulder. Orange-yellow flames shot from the smoke. Crackling and hissing filled the air as the firefighters moved back.

She shifted toward Alex and said, "I don't—"

An explosion of bright blue white light shook the ground, throwing her against Alex, all words fleeing her mind.

TWO

Alex grasped Rebecca as a wall of dark smoke and flames rose behind the Outdoor Sports and Recreation store. He held her trembling body for a few seconds as she gathered her composure before he grabbed her hand and tugged her toward the front parking lot.

She took a few steps then halted. "But what if—"

Alex turned back. Rebecca was used to being in charge. "We need to let the fire department deal with the situation. These kind of fires are extremely dangerous."

Dressed in black pants and matching jacket with a white blouse, she was all business as though she regretted a moment of weakness after the transformer exploded. He started to tell her a strand was loose from her bun, but her mouth pinched in a thin line as though she were mulling over her options. She smoothed her hand over her dark brown hair, found the stray strand and frowned, as if she wasn't sure what to do with it.

Alex tucked the errant strand into her loose knot of curls at the back of her head then clasped her elbow and started again for the front of the store. She took independence to the extreme, and he understood why. When Clint went into the U.S. Marines, she was the only one left for her father to school in running the company. He'd been a hard taskmaster, honing her into a tough executive. The determined girl who used to hang around Clint and Alex had always tried to live up to her father's expectations. Clint had dealt with that by leaving and joining the marines. Alex knew the pressures of family members. He dealt with his own concerning his mother and younger siblings.

When they emerged from the right side of the building, Rebecca shook loose of his hold and increased her pace to Clint, who was talking to Officer Josh Mills with his Rottweiler K-9, Bruno, next to him.

When Alex approached the trio, Rebecca asked Josh, "Is it safe to go back inside?"

"We still have a team upstairs on the fourth floor. No evidence of a bomb so far. I heard the blast out back. Did the transformer blow?"

"Yes," Alex said before Rebecca had a chance. "Everyone needs to stay out of the building until the fire's put out. Electricity can be unpredictable." If the wind blew in the wrong direction, that would put the store in danger of catching fire. "Recall the remaining team. I don't want them trapped inside if there's a problem. They can finish after it's safe."

Rebecca panned the parking lot. "Where's George?"

"He's with the team on the fourth floor." Josh stepped away to communicate with them.

"We won't be able to reopen, Rebecca, until the transformer is replaced at the very least and the computers are back up. Our generator only handles things needed in an emergency." Clint waved to Neil to join him.

Neil finished his discussion with the members of his department and came their way.

"I know. This is a busy time for us with the Thanksgiving weekend coming up. We need to get back up and running as soon as possible." Rebecca shifted her attention to Alex. "I want answers to what happened here today."

"And I intend to get them, but if these two incidents occurring five minutes apart weren't an accident, whoever's behind this is after something, perhaps connected to the computer system. If we discover what, it'll help me narrow down who did this. At this point we don't even know if it's one person or more."

Neil stopped next to Clint. "Since the network of computers went down before the power outage, I agree that must be the main target. When my team can get back inside and investigate what happened, we'll be able to see what damage was done and how."

Rebecca straightened. "What do you think it is?"

"As I said earlier, it could be a virus or malware in the system. It could be someone hacking into our network to look for certain information."

Rebecca curled her hands at her side. "Financial and credit info?"

"Most likely." Neil frowned.

"Okay. We need to presume the worst and pray for the best. Gather your people, Neil. We'll meet in the original store in ten minutes. It's far enough away from the transformer that we should be safe." Rebecca gestured toward the small building that still stood fifty yards from the main one and not in the direction the wind was blowing.

"I'll get George and some of his security team." Clint swung around then walked toward the men coming out of the building.

"We also need our advertising

department in the meeting."

Her brother glanced over his shoulder. "I'll take care of it."

Rebecca started for the original Outdoor Sports and Recreation, determination in every tense line of her body.

"Josh, come with me." Alex strode in the direction Rebecca was going and called out, "Wait up, Rebecca."

She halted and pivoted. "Do what you need, Alex. I've got to get ahead of this situation with my staff. We're heavily invested in this big celebration starting on Black Friday, not to mention the holiday season officially starting that day."

"Not until Josh and I check this building."

The color drained from her cheeks. "You think something's wrong with it." She gestured toward the old store. "It hasn't been used in several years other than for storage."

"Humor me, Rebecca." Alex passed her and kept heading for the entrance.

As he drew closer, he searched the front façade for any sign someone might be inside. The original store was in a one-story, red brick structure approximately five thousand square feet. He waited for Rebecca to give him the key.

She stuffed her hand into her jacket pocket and withdrew a large ring full of keys. As she flipped through them, she glanced at Bruno then Alex. "Do you think someone planted a bomb in this building? Why would they?"

"It's close, so maybe. It's a good place to spy on the store. Mainly, I'm checking as a precaution. Don't assume anything. I learned that the hard way." Years ago his partner and he had assumed a place was safe because it didn't seem logical as a hideout, and Brad had ended up shot in the chest. Permanently disabled because his right lung was removed, his partner had ended up leaving the police force. For the past ten years, Alex had regretted agreeing with Brad.

After Alex unlocked the door, he opened it and motioned Josh and Bruno inside. "You stay outside, Rebecca, away from the building until I tell you it's clear. Make sure everyone does."

She nodded.

As Alex moved through the musty building in a clockwise direction, he removed his gun from its holster while Josh directed Bruno to check out each area, smelling for a bomb. The quiet and stillness didn't sway Alex to hurry the search. He'd done enough of these to expect the unexpected.

At the back of the large open space where the store had been, Bruno growled, a low menacing sound. Josh unhooked the dog's leash and commanded him to find whatever was putting him on alert. No words were spoken, but Alex had been with Josh and the Rottweiler enough to know what the signals meant.

Bruno took off with Josh and Alex following the dog into a large office. Stacked boxes flanked the room with a big desk and chair in the middle, but what riveted Alex's attention was a windowsill, wiped clean of the thick layer of dust covering the rest of the place. The Rottweiler charged toward the desk.

Alex rounded it.

A bearded man lay on a sleeping bag, his eyes closed.

While Josh commanded Bruno to guard, Alex approached the person, his gun aimed at him. The stench that rose from the dirty clothes, coupled with the smell of alcohol, assailed Alex's senses. He nudged the drunk who groaned and rolled to his side.

"I don't think he's our guy, but maybe he knows something." Alex holstered his gun while Josh kept his aimed at the man. When Alex pulled one arm behind the drunk's back, the man rallied. Quickly Alex handcuffed him before he came completely awake. Then he rolled the vagrant over, facing the floor.

"What's—goin' on?" the drunk slurred his words, trying to lift his head to see around him but it was too much of an effort to hold it up.

"You're under arrest for trespassing and loitering." Alex took the man's arms and helped him to stand. The vagrant swayed until Alex steadied him, close to his body. The odor reeking from the man overpowered Alex's senses.

The drunk's bloodshot eyes widened when he spied Bruno. He scrambled away until the back of his legs hit the desk. With Alex and Josh on each side of the man and Bruno in front, he was trapped. The vagrant glanced at the window behind the Rottweiler.

"Don't even think it." Alex took hold of his right arm and started for the exit. "Josh, finish the sweep while I take care of this one."

"I ain't done nuthin' wrong." The older man faltered, but Alex caught him before he went down.

"You broke into this place. That's against the law."

"Nope, it was open." The guy stumbled over his own two feet and fell into a stack of boxes. His eyes slid close for a few seconds then popped open, a confused expression in them.

Again Alex righted him and kept moving toward the exit. The smell pouring off of his charge indicated he hadn't had a bath in months. Alex's gut roiled. When he stepped out in the crisp, cold air, he signaled to a patrol officer. "Officer Bailey, take him to jail and have them let me know when he's sober enough to carry on a conversation—and clean."

After the drunk was escorted to the officer's cruiser, Rebecca came up to Alex. "He was inside? How? The front door was locked. The back one wasn't?"

"It was. He got in through a window."

"He broke a window?"

"No."

"It should have been locked. I have security check this building weekly to make sure."

"I'm going to talk to him. Then I'll let you know. He said it was open, but then he's also drunk, and I'm not sure he even knows where he is."

When Josh emerged from the building, he gave the all-clear sign.

Alex looked into Rebecca's blue eyes, the color of a storm brewing in the Bering Sea. "It's okay for you and your employees to go inside, but there has to be a better place to meet."

"Yeah, my conference room, but we can't go inside yet. I don't want to leave the site until the fire is out, and I can do a walkthrough with some of my key personnel."

"That could be hours."

"I know but our store needs to be open in two days, the day before Thanksgiving. If I have to work around the clock, I will. We have a big promotion with the mushers who we're sponsoring this year in the Iditarod Race. It's already been widely publicized for the past couple of weeks. I prefer not canceling."

Knowing Rebecca, he had to ask, "Are you going to sleep at the store tonight?"

"Yes, with extra security posted at all exits. I'll be safe."

As groups of employees streamed into the old store, Alex noted each one. This could have been an inside job. He couldn't rule that out. "If they're after the credit information and hacked into the computer system, then that's the reason for what happened today. There shouldn't be any more problems." He hoped.

"If they got it. Neil will have to determine that."

"And we can't assume that's the reason for what's behind this." An uneasiness nagged at Alex. "I'll touch base with you here later, especially after I talk with the vagrant. Will Clint be with you?"

"Yes, and he's just as good as you at protecting his loved ones."

"You'd better go." Alex gestured toward Clint standing in the entrance. "See you later."

As Rebecca disappeared inside, the hairs on Alex's nape tingled a warning. He slowly rotated, taking in his surroundings. Although Outdoor Sports and Recreation sat on a large piece of land, it was located near the downtown area with lots of other businesses nearby. Plenty of places to hide and watch what was going on.

* * *

Rebecca peered out the large window behind her desk, her body past exhaustion. Every muscle protested as though she'd raced in the Iditarod. The finish line in Nome was in her line of vision—except this wasn't the end of the ordeal that occurred today at the store. Neil left her office a few minutes ago after informing her that whoever was in their system didn't use a computer in the building, and likely their list of customers and their credit card information were accessed because a virus was planted in that part of the data. Also some of the security footage for the past couple of days had been erased, which made her think the intruder had been somehow caught on the tape, unlike the incident last week on the main floor of the store. That culprit had managed to avoid the cameras, which made her wonder how much he'd cased the store before releasing the stink bomb. Were the two events even related?

Though not surprised, she hadn't wanted to hear that the credit card numbers had been accessed. Money was a great motivator for some people—at least that was Clint's take on it. She wasn't so sure. If so, then why take out the transformer? To give whoever was behind all of this time to go through the network and grab what they wanted without one of her employees detecting it? Chaos certainly occurred with the power outage. George said there had been multiple bullets shot at it earlier until one sparked the fire. It hadn't gone up in flames for a while, but it had disrupted the power. The worst part was no one heard or saw anything out back, but then there were several places a person could hide, and a silencer would have helped dampen the sound.

Note to self: put extra cameras in the back with one trained on the new transformer, hopefully being installed tomorrow if the piece of equipment arrived on the jet she hired to bring it to Anchorage. The size she needed wasn't currently available in the state. She was thankful the electric company was working with her on this situation. She would also put a concrete wall around the transformer to prevent a similar attack in the future.

She leaned against the window, relishing the coldness seeping through the glass. An SUV pulled into the large, near empty parking lot below. Alex was here. Her pulse rate picked up as her mind flooded with images of him helping her earlier from the elevator then later when the transformer finally exploded.

Maybe he would have more answers for her than questions. Her head throbbed with them. In the light of the security lamp in the parking lot, he climbed from his gray SUV, which reminded her of the color of his eyes. The wind still blew and messed with his dark brown hair, cut short.

Suddenly he glanced up at her. His step slowed. Even from a distance she felt as though his gaze had seized hers and held it captive. Her knees weakened, and she leaned more against the windowsill. Finally, Alex looked away and resumed his trek toward the entrance.

Watching him disappear inside, she remembered all the times they had worked together on searches and rescues. She'd known him for years, but he'd always held part of himself back. While growing up, he'd become the father figure in his family after his dad, a police officer, had been killed in the line of duty. He had a younger sister and brother, and when his mother fell apart after her husband's death, he stepped up and took over for her. He'd only been twelve. After that she saw less of him. But when her brother returned to Anchorage, dealing with post-traumatic stress after being held as a prisoner of war, Alex had been there for him as a friend who listened. Clint had needed that. Alex was the one who had gotten Clint interested in being part of a search and rescue team—actually both of them—because she joined an Anchorage SAR group, too.

Rebecca crossed to her leather couch and sank onto It, almost afraid to give into its comfort. That reaction to Alex a moment ago was only due to the stress of the past day. That was all. Laying her head on the back cushion, she closed her eyes to unwind for a few minutes before seeing him again and plunging into work.

She drifted toward the darkness, sucking her in like a whirlpool in the ocean.

Someone shook her arm. She jolted straight up on the couch, ready to protect herself—until she looked into Alex's gleaming eyes, laugh lines fanning out from the corners of them.

He drew away and settled on the couch at the other end. "You must be as tired as I am. I almost didn't wake you, but then I figured you wouldn't be too happy with me for that."

"You know me well. Do you have any leads?"

"The drunk we found insists he came through an unlocked window to get out of the cold and to sleep."

"Do you believe him?"

"Yes. This isn't the first time Sam Dickerson has done that with other places. Not to mention the amount of alcohol in his system would have made it hard for him to pull off the shooting and hacking into the computer, even if he had the skill to do so. What little I can find out about the man supports that."

"George personally checks the old building each week. He's been with the company a long time and started out working at the original store. Everything was locked up as of two days ago."

"Does he check it the same day each week?"

"Yes, but the times vary."

"So someone could have gotten into the building during those two days."

"I admit the security isn't as strong there as it is at the new store, but why would someone want in it?"

"They're close enough to your computer network that they might be able to hack into your system unseen. In a car in the parking lot, the person could be caught on camera or at least a license plate number could be captured. Tomorrow, I'm going back to check the old building and see if I can find where he might have set up. I want George to go with me."

"Sure. I'll let him know. When do you want to do it?"

"I'll call you in the morning. But the earlier the better."

She released a long sigh.

"Go home, Rebecca. You need rest. You

said yourself that this is a busy time for you and the business. You'll function better with sleep. Is the store still going to be closed tomorrow?"

"Yes, but I'm determined it will open on Wednesday. As a sponsor, the Iditarod promotion is important. It's a big event here in March, and I want to start our build up during the holiday season."

"And how will you manage it if you keep falling asleep like you were when I came in?"

"I'm afraid I might fall asleep on the drive home, so I'm going to make do with this couch." She patted the brown leather cushion between them.

"I know you have a few security guards on duty tonight, but go home. I'll drive you. I have to be back here early tomorrow, so I'll pick you up. Your house is on my way."

A laugh bubbled up in her, and it felt good. "Yeah, if you go five miles out of your way."

"Another good idea is to bring Susie with you tomorrow."

"I was thinking about that."

"See, you need to go home to get Susie so you might as well stay there for the night."

"You are persistent."

"It helps when I have a difficult case to solve."

Rebecca panned the office, the urge to leave if only for a few hours overwhelming her. Why did she think sleeping here would prove she was a good CEO? She couldn't change what happened earlier today, and certainly her tossing and turning on a narrow couch wasn't going to help her to be rested for tomorrow's grueling work. Even now her father's influence governed her actions. She still tried to please him even though he wasn't around to see it.

She gave Alex a small smile. "Your power of persuasion has swayed me."

"A wise woman. Are you ready to leave?"

"Yes." She rose, gathered her coat and purse, and left the office with him. "Let's take the stairs. I'm going back to using them rather than the elevator."

"An elevator isn't a refrigerator that doesn't open from the inside."

"I beg to differ. I couldn't open the elevator door when I tried earlier." As she descended the stairs four floors, she slanted a glance at Alex. "You're one of the few people who knows about my fear."

"And I won't tell anyone."

She paused on a step and really assessed the man she'd known for years and yet hadn't. Not deep inside. But what she did know was that he was a loyal friend and very good at his job. "I never thought you would." In the dim light, she resumed her descent. She trusted Alex as much as she did her twin brother. "I knew rationally I would be saved from the elevator, but that didn't make any difference when I couldn't get the door open. My emotions took over, and I couldn't stop them." And she didn't like the fact that they had. "Are you afraid of anything?"

Alex waited to answer until after they left the store. "Every time I confront a suspect there's a tiny part of me that wants to flee. I wonder if I'll die like my dad when he answered a call about a domestic dispute between a husband and wife. That man opened the door and blasted my father with a shotgun before he even had a chance to draw his gun. That image runs through my mind at odd times."

"Why are you a police officer then?" Rebecca slipped into his SUV, releasing some of the tension gripping her as she put distance between her and the store.

"I loved hearing my dad talk about his job and how he was helping others. He could never talk to Mom about his work, but he did with me. We were close. His death changed my life."

Her parents' deaths had affected her even though she'd never been close to her father in a warm fuzzy way. But she still felt he was watching every move she made, ready to criticize her if she didn't do it his way. Even after six years being solely in charge of the company, she questioned everything she did. More and more, she was moving in what she thought was the right direction while she fought that little voice telling her she was wrong—her father would want her to do it differently.

"My dad's death changed mine, too, but not in the way yours did." Even from the grave his disapproval weighed her down. In tough situations like today, she wondered when she'd be free to live her life. So many people's livelihood depended on her decisions and moves. At the moment, in her weariness, she wished otherwise. Tomorrow, she would be ready to fight back.

"You didn't want to run Outdoor Sports and Recreation?" Alex drove out of the parking lot.

"Yes and no." She slowly relaxed the more distance put between her and the store. "I'll deny this tomorrow, but tonight I don't want to make one more decision. I don't want to be responsible for hundreds of employees. Worry if they will be safe or my customers' credit information will be protected. I see my friends in their jobs helping people, and in Laura's case, caring for animals as a veterinarian. Tory runs the search and rescue organization. They see how they affect others' lives. What I do doesn't really help others."

"Are you feeling sorry for yourself? This is new." Alex stopped at a red light and peered at her. "You're always in control, tough."

"That's just it. I don't want to be—at least until tomorrow. I've been working for sixteen hours and dealing with one crisis after another. This is only the beginning." Rebecca took in the dark, deserted streets at one in the morning. "I have a feeling whoever did this isn't through."

"Yeah, so do I." He crossed the intersection.

She angled toward him. "And you didn't say anything to me about that? Did you find something to make you feel that way?"

"Not exactly, but I've been a police officer for fifteen years, and occasionally, I get a gut feeling about a case that there's more to it and so far I've never been wrong."

"I'm hoping in this situation you are."

"So am I."

"My family doesn't need any more angst after what happened to Clint, Tory, and me last year when that stalker came after Tory. That's enough adventure for my lifetime."

"I agree. I almost lost three good friends that day."

His words warmed her. They reminded her she had people who cared about her and wanted the best for her. Like Clint earlier today. When had she set aside some time for herself? Clint wanted her to take a vacation before the actual Iditarod Race took place. Maybe, for once, she needed to heed his advice. He was certainly capable of running the company while she lay on a beach in Hawaii. "When did you last take a vacation?"

"Christmas—last year."

"But you stayed here. When was the last time you totally got away from Anchorage for more than a couple of days? You and Clint go camping some, but that's over the weekend and doesn't count."

"You mean a complete change of scenery?"

She punched the remote to open the black iron gates to her property. "Yes."

"I'd say about ten years ago. My family can be demanding of my time when I'm not working. Two siblings with six kids between them and a mother who constantly needs my help."

"How?"

"The last time she got her bank account in a mess."

"Do your brother and sister step in and help her at times?"

"That'll be the day. Mark is almost as bad as Mom with finances. Thankfully, Beth's husband does their checkbook." Alex parked in front of her large gray stone house. "Math has never been my strong suit, but somehow I ended up doing the job with my family."

"Thanks for bringing me home. I need to be at the store by seven," she checked the clock in the dashboard and groaned, "in five and a half hours." She dug into her purse and pulled out the remote. "In the morning use this to get in the gate." She opened the passenger door and climbed out.

When she straightened, Alex exited the

car on his side, scanning the front of the house. "It's dark. Don't Martha and Henry stay in the house?"

The couple took care of her home and property. They had done those tasks for years since she was a child. "No. I'm surprised the front porch light isn't on though. They always leave it on for me."

Alex rounded the hood. "That's okay. I'll walk you to the door. The light bulb might be out."

Rebecca shone her flashlight on her cell phone as she moved to the porch. The bright glow fell onto the massive wooden door with a white paper, flapping in the breeze, pinned to it.

Rebecca's stomach churned as she closed the distance to the sheet. She normally didn't use this entrance but the one in the garage. When she reached for the note, Alex leaned around and stopped her.

"Don't."

THREE

Alex moved in front of Rebecca. There were two pieces of paper—a vaguely worded note on the top and a database listing on the bottom one—tacked to the door. "Don't touch it. Let me handle this."

She peeked around him and waved her hand toward the sheets. "Who put this here?"

Alex retrieved a pair of latex gloves from his pocket and carefully unpinned the message while Rebecca came around and shone her light on it. When he shuffled the top page to the bottom, it revealed a database listing.

Rebecca sucked in a gasp. "That's credit

card information for a list of people I'm not familiar with."

Alex looked up and searched the darkness beyond the porch. "Let's get inside and see if this has anything to do with what was stolen from your network." The sensation of being watched bore into him as strongly as it had when he came out of the old store earlier.

Rebecca passed him her cell phone while she rummaged for her keys in a large black leather purse. "Honestly, I need a keeper."

"I thought you were always so organized."

"I am except for some reason not my handbag. Its size keeps growing bigger each year as I have more to carry around. Remember in high school, I hated having a purse. That feeling hasn't changed." She withdrew the key and tried to stick it in upside down.

Alex returned her cell phone and took over opening her door. "Let's get inside."

Rebecca glanced over her shoulder. "If this wasn't from Clint, Martha, or Henry,

49

and they wouldn't put it here, then that means someone most likely climbed over the fence to put this on my door. Why would they go to all that trouble? What's going on?" Her voice quavered.

"We'll talk about it in a minute. Where's Susie? Where are Martha and Henry?" Alex shoved the door all the way open, the beeping of her alarm filling the air.

Rebecca hurried into the house. "Susie's probably in her kennel. When I'm not here at night, Henry puts her in there before he and his wife retire to the cabin out back."

"Oh, that's right." When Clint and Tory moved to their new house, the Sterns decided to live in the cabin. "Maybe you should ask them to come back until this is over."

Rebecca quickly tapped the security code in the box near the front door, and the noise died. "I can't. For the past year, they've had very little alone time. When I suggested they take the cabin after Clint left, they jumped at it."

"So you're here alone?"

"When I'm here, I have Susie, and she's

great company."

"Where's her kennel?"

"Off the kitchen." Rebecca headed for the back of the house. "I'll let her out. She'd be barking if there was an intruder."

"Bring two plastic bags for me to put these papers in."

"Okay."

While he waited for Rebecca to return, he moved into the formal living room, remembering the times he'd been here in the past, especially when Tory was in danger and Clint watched over her. Rebecca might need protection, but she wouldn't likely go for it. He held up the first page of the sheets and read it.

Rebecca, I thought you should know.

Know what? Although the words weren't menacing, that was the feeling he got when he read the note.

He examined the database page. The information on ten people was most likely from the computer system at the store confirming what Neil suspected. Not good news for the company.

At the sound of footsteps approaching

from the back of the house, he swung around and faced the entrance into the living room. Rebecca entered with Susie by her side. Tired eyes and a solemn expression highlighted Rebecca's weariness. He wished he could keep this from her until she rested, but she'd already seen it and would want answers. She wouldn't go to sleep until she inspected the information on the sheets more closely.

Susie made a beeline for him, her tail wagging. Mostly black with tan markings, Susie was a German shepherd that at times he thought understood everything being said around her. He patted her and rubbed his hand down her back. She loved that.

"She's missed seeing you." Rebecca presented him with the large plastic bags. After Alex carefully slipped each page into one, Rebecca held her hand out for them. She studied the database sheet first then the note, her frown lines deepening the longer she looked at them. "I can't stay here. Neil is at the store working with his IT team. I need to know if this is our customers' credit card information from the store."

"But you should rest first," he said, even though it would be useless to say.

"I couldn't sleep if I wanted. Will you take me back to the store? I don't expect you to stay, but these people will need to be informed first thing this morning."

"Tell you what. I'll drive back to the store and give this to Neil while you at least try to rest."

Rebecca settled her balled hand on her waist. "Alex Kincaid, I'll call a cab if I have to. I do need to take a shower and change because I don't know when I'll be back."

He wanted to argue with her, but the stubborn set of her mouth as well as her narrowed gaze told him she wouldn't listen. She wouldn't admit that the episode in the elevator drained her emotionally. He still could recall her as a nine-year-old flying out of that refrigerator into his arms, clinging to him, her sweaty body shaking, her tears soaking his shirt. Seeing her in a moment of vulnerability had troubled him, too.

When he didn't reply right away, she

said, "Okay. After I talk with Neil, I'll lie down on the couch in my office and try to get some rest. Also, I'll take Susie with me. No one could get into my office with her guarding me. That's all I can promise."

"Okay, but I'm staying, too."

She opened her mouth, but instead of saying something, she snapped it closed and whirled around. "I'll be back in fifteen minutes. Then we'll leave. Susie will keep you company."

After the creepy feeling he'd gotten from examining the note in detail, he didn't want her to be alone even in her house. "No. You take her, and I'll walk you to your room."

She looked back at him, one eyebrow lifted. "If someone was in this house besides us, Susie would let me know. I'm fine."

As she and her dog walked from the living room, Alex gritted his teeth. Her father had demanded she be tough, and over the years, under her dad's tutelage, he'd seen a hard exterior encase what he knew was a tender heart. He remembered every injured animal she needed to help, and if abandoned, she wanted to take it in. Then after Cade died, she withdrew into a shell. She worked all the time, especially after her parents died in the small airplane crash. When Clint came back with his German shepherd, Sitka, it was the first time she'd gotten a pet in years. She and Clint trained their dogs for search and rescue missions, and slowly he'd begun to see glimpses of the young girl he'd known.

* * *

A growl penetrated Rebecca's dream world. She jerked upright on her office couch, blinking rapidly as her eyes adjusted to the overhead light she'd left on. She glanced at the window, and it was still dark outside. This time of year daylight was short.

A rap at the door awakened her fully, and she swung her feet to the carpeted floor and hurried to answer the second knock, a little louder than the first. Susie padded forward, a low rumble still emitting from her, and planted herself between her and the entrance, as though waiting for it to open so she could attack an intruder. Susie sensed something was wrong. Her dog didn't usually come to the store with her.

"Susie, calm down. If it were a bad guy, he wouldn't knock. Sit."

She whined but did what Rebecca commanded. Her dog felt Rebecca's tension and was ready to defend her.

Rebecca skirted Susie, saying, "Good girl," and opened the door.

Alex stood with two cups of coffee and a bag from a bagel shop she loved. "I hope you're hungry. I went out and made a run for breakfast. I brought you two of your favorite bagels—cinnamon and blueberry."

Rebecca's stomach gurgled as she stepped to the side. "I can't believe it's seven already. I feel like I just shut my eyes."

"Seven? It's eight."

Rebecca took the bag from him and glanced at her watch. "I told Neil to have someone wake me up at seven."

"I think your brother overrode that.

Now I understand why Clint was so eager for me to get you up. He didn't want to face your wrath."

"I'll save it for him. Did you get any sleep on my brother's office couch?"

"About two hours. I went home and changed then stopped for breakfast."

She smiled and moved to her round table across the room from the sofa. "One of my favorite places to pick up something to eat on the way to work. Thank you. I know you went out of your way to get this." She shook the sack.

"How about you? Any rest?"

She chuckled. "You were right last night when you told me I practically was sleepwalking. The second my head hit the cushion I was out. I didn't even turn off the overhead light."

"And you got an extra hour of rest. Good."

As Rebecca laid the six wrapped bagels and tubs of cream cheese on the table, she lifted her head. "I'm hungry, but I can't eat three of these."

"Clint is joining us in a few minutes.

He's seeing to the transformer being delivered here. I already gave him his coffee."

"I don't know if I would have slept if I hadn't found out the equipment made its flight. At least I won't have to rearrange the promotional event planned tomorrow at the store."

"I saw some of your employees starting to set up the display and decorating for the event. What time does it start? What security precautions have you taken?"

"I'm glad you brought that up. George is beefing up security for tomorrow, but we're looking into other long-term measures, too. Would you consult with George on tomorrow's activities? I know this isn't your job, but I'll pay you for your services."

"No." He paused and sipped his coffee. "I can't accept money from a good friend. I'll do it for free, and knowing my captain, I have a feeling he'll breathe easier if I attend and personally keep an eye out for any trouble."

"They've already gotten what they

wanted—credit card information on our customers. We're notifying every credit company involved. I'll be issuing a statement to the press this afternoon after we get in touch with as many customers as we can. We've taken the computers with the financial information offline for the time being, and we're strengthening our firewalls. I have computer consultants meeting with me, Clint, and Neil after lunch. So do you still think something could happen tomorrow? Why would they risk it?"

"I can't assume they might not do anything. I have to plan as if they will. Proper security is always formulated with that notion. Most of the time it's unnecessary, but the few times it is, good security saves lives and property."

"Will you be able to work with George after our conference meeting this morning?"

"I have to go into the station, but I should be able to talk to him after that."

"When will you know about fingerprints on the sheets of paper on my door?"

"I already do. Nothing usable."

"I'm considering electrifying my fence to deter anyone else climbing over it. Not sure why someone would do that. It's not like they didn't leave enough tracks in our computer system to announce what they did."

"As though they wanted you to find out what they did right away. Interesting."

Tension in her neck and shoulders spread as if her spine was a rope knotted all the way down her back. "Why do you say that?"

"There may be more going on than what's obvious."

"Like what?"

"They're planning to attack more stores and businesses. Our security systems and methods are often twentieth century while the criminals are way ahead of the game. And often hackers think this is a game. Or something else besides money is motivating them. Do you know of anyone that has a grudge against you or Outdoor Sports and Recreation?"

"Like someone who was fired?"

"Maybe."

Rebecca kneaded the side of her neck. "Here at this store I haven't personally fired anyone lately. I don't usually do it. We have protocols and procedures in place. It goes through personnel now."

"Sometimes when a person has a grievance against another, it doesn't always make sense to anyone else. That's why we have to think of all possibilities, or we'll miss it."

She'd always known Alex was good at his job, but after seeing him at work on the case involving Tory and Clint last year and now this one, she was impressed. This was a whole different side to him. Even tired from long hours, he came across as confident and in control. Hunger rumbled her stomach. She slathered cream cheese on her cinnamon bagel and took a bite.

"How are your mother and siblings doing?" Rebecca asked, needing for a short time to put the current situation to the side and enjoy her breakfast with someone she cared about.

"My little brother is doing well as a patrol officer. He got a promotion. My mother keeps hoping he'll do something else. Even after working on the police force for fifteen years, she pesters me to quit and get a normal—in other words, a safe—job. My sister lives with Mom now, which means I have to referee between them a couple of times a week."

"Your family keeps you busy."

"More than I signed on for. Most of their bickering is petty. Between my job and family, I'm kept busy."

"I know the feeling, but mainly it's my company that demands my time. When I do something with Clint and his family, it's a break. I love being around my nephew."

"Didn't you once say you wanted children? I was surprised you and Cade didn't have any."

If other people had asked that question, she would have shut down immediately, but Alex knew her better than most, even at times more than Clint because her brother had left Alaska for ten years. Alex stayed. "My plans changed." She would need a husband for that, and she'd failed at her marriage with Cade. She didn't repeat mistakes. To the world, they had been happy, and they were for a while, but deep inside she knew she'd let Cade down those last few years when her father demanded all of her time. She'd always wanted to run the business, but she could only do it on her dad's terms. "My company takes a lot of time."

"What I've seen in response to the situation yesterday was good. Your different departments and the people who run them are well organized."

"But you have to be constantly on top of everything and everyone. That takes time."

"Did you personally hire your department heads?"

"Most of them. A few I inherited from my father."

"Do you trust your judgment?"

"I know where this is headed. You think I should let go of some of my responsibilities and let the others do their job. But mine is supervising the whole company. I look at the big picture."

His mouth quirked into a grin. "Do you

love your job?"

"Yes—usually."

"Then you're doing what you want. You can't ask for more than that."

But she wanted more, or at least at one time she had. She was beginning to question what she wanted now. "So one workaholic to another, do you love your job?"

"Yes—usually." His smile expanded to encompass his whole expression, down to the gleam in his eyes.

"Well, no job is perfect. The challenges keep my work interesting."

"Rarely is being a detective boring. But mostly it fulfills something deep inside me, especially when I help bring someone to justice like the serial bomber last year."

"Or finding the guy trying to kidnap kids last year."

Alex shifted on his chair as if he were uncomfortable with the accolades. Like so many who took part in the Anchorage SAR group, he liked to stay in the background and do what he could without people knowing.

She patted his hand nearest her. "You need to accept that you're a hero in a lot of people's eyes."

"Who is OSR sponsoring in this year's Iditarod Race?"

Rebecca laughed, glad she could in the midst of the current crisis. "You are not good at subtlety. But I'll respect your wishes and not talk about what you do well. We're sponsoring two different mushers, a man and woman, Brian Nanuq and Kimberly Moore, as well as signing on as an overall sponsor of the race."

"You might have a winner. Both are formidable."

"I hope one of them is." Rebecca started to take another bite of her bagel, but the phone on her desk rang. "Excuse me." She rushed to answer it, hoping this wasn't any bad news about the transformer. "Hello."

"Sis, I found something. You and Alex need to come to the first floor by the tents ASAP."

FOUR

"What's that?" Rebecca stood in the outdoor camping section of the store on the first floor.

Alex donned one latex glove and carefully picked up the black box that had been placed inside a display tent. "It's a cell phone jammer. That would explain why are phones weren't working yesterday. Who found this?"

"Heather Adams." Clint waved for an employee to join them.

"She was the cashier Matt Pinkston harassed a few months ago."

Although not a question, Clint nodded. "She works hard. Today she's been helping us get ready for tomorrow's Iditarod promo since we aren't open for business."

While smiling at the young woman with short, spikey, blond hair and a shy demeanor, Rebecca shook her hand. "It's good to see you again. Are you still getting those secret admirer notes?"

"The last one was a couple of weeks ago. My boyfriend hasn't been too happy about them." Heather met Rebecca's eyes briefly then lowered her gaze to a spot on the floor between them.

"I know you mentioned getting a restraining order against Matt Pinkston. You should look into it." Rebecca gestured toward the black box. "Thank you for pointing this out to my brother. Now we know how the phones were jammed."

"Just doing my job."

"Are you working tomorrow?"

"Yes."

"Good. We need an alert staff."

After Heather went back to assisting another employee setting up the sled Kimberly Moore would use in the Iditarod Race, Rebecca turned to Alex. "Maybe there'll be latent prints on it."

"Possibly. I'll check with Miss Adams to get her fingerprints so I can rule her out. We'll try to track down where this was bought, but with so many things being purchased online, it might be a dead end."

"I think all she touched was the handle. That's how she brought it to me. She thought it was something that belonged in another department. Should we be looking for more?" Clint asked, scanning the store.

Alex lifted the box and examined it. "Maybe, but this looks like a cell phone jammer we've used on the job. I'll check to make sure, but if so, it blocks a signal up to half a mile, which would cover the whole place. Are there surveillance cameras that would have caught the person planting this on tape?"

"Not on this exact spot. With the power off, most of the cameras went down, so I don't know how much they'll show you. George is already making copies of the security tapes we have from yesterday that weren't erased, but I'll also have him do the day before. He'll get it to you after lunch." So many things had changed since Rebecca had been a part of the company her father started. The measures a store had to take to keep a safe environment for their customers had multiplied exponentially in the twenty-five years Outdoor Sports and Recreation had been first opened.

Clint frowned. "I wish we could search everyone coming into the store tomorrow, but a store doesn't get to use that extra security measure. As a customer, I wouldn't want to have to wait in line while other people are checked, just to get inside so I can spend my money." He sighed. "I'd better get back to work, especially on organizing the parking lot for Brian Nanuq's demonstration on being a musher. The kids will love that."

"My nephew sure would. If I need any more info, I know where you'll be, Clint." Alex faced Rebecca. "I know this isn't a good time, but I could use someone to help me ID customers and employees on the tapes."

"Sadly, I probably couldn't do that with

how fast the company has grown in the last five years, but for this store, George or someone in security should be able to. Tell you what. Instead of taking the security footage to your police station, let me set something up this afternoon in my conference room for you and whoever you want to go through the tapes. That way I can have a person from George's department assisting you, and if I get a chance, I'll help when not dealing with all the last minute details."

"I'm going to take this evidence to the station. Then I'll be back. I'll feel better if I'm familiar with your security measures for tomorrow."

"I could use all the help you'll give us. I'm hiring extra security for the event and the gala in eleven days. It's important nothing goes wrong."

"I won't be long. I'm hoping some evidence can be pulled from this jammer." He started toward the front of the store.

Rebecca kept pace with him. "I could use a breath of fresh air before I go back to my office."

Alex opened the main door. Then in the entrance blocked her path. "Stay inside as much as you can. I don't like you even standing here. We don't know what's going on."

"Yes, we do. Someone has it in for Outdoor Sports and Recreation. Everything has been aimed at the store."

"Then after the promotion tomorrow, we need to dig into who would feel that way. I'd say we should consider competitors, too, but there aren't any since your big expansion push five years ago. I won't rule that angle out if nothing else pans out though." He grasped her upper arm. "I won't stop until I find who's behind this."

"Thanks. That means a lot to me."

Alex let the door swish closed.

He walked toward his SUV not far from the entrance.

She'd always given people the benefit of doubt before making a decision to fire them, at least when she'd handled that personally before she took over running the business six years ago. Now there were procedures in place to deal with employee issues from thief to improper performance of duties. She'd have to look back through the records to figure out who she'd fired. But then, if it was a case of her firing the person who was behind the current incidents, why would he or she have waited this long to get back at her? No, it must have to do with the company.

Rebecca swung around and headed for the staircase to the fourth floor. As she mounted the steps, the sound of her footfalls echoed through the concrete shaft. Usually there were other people here, but without customers, only part of the employees had been called in today. She paused at the third floor door. Maybe she should go by and talk to George first.

The quiet surrounding her gave her chills that had nothing to do with the cool temperature in the stairwell. Then suddenly footsteps below her intruded into the silence. She grabbed the knob and hurried down the hall to the head of security's office. Her first reaction—fear—to the sound angered her. Her father had thought fear was a useless emotion that hindered people from acting the way they should—in control and capable of handling anything. There was a guard at each entrance into the building and only about forty people inside, all people she knew. Running on little sleep was making her overreact.

* * *

"Not too much longer and this will be over with, and you can breathe again," Alex whispered to Rebecca, off to the side of the platform set up inside the store for Kimberly Moore.

She turned her head toward him, their faces only a few inches apart. For a moment, the people around her faded from her view, and all she could focus on was Alex's beautiful silver-gray eyes. They drew her in. Her heartbeat reacted, kicking up a notch. She dragged her attention downward, latching onto his mouth. Instantly, she realized that was a mistake.

She stepped back, but she couldn't shake the question dominating her thoughts. What would it be like to be kissed by Alex? What was going on? He'd been a good friend to her for years. She, Clint, and Alex had been a threesome as kids.

She quickly swiveled away from him and concentrated on Kimberly, thanking her company for sponsoring her in the Iditarod Race. The two mushers' appearances at OSR had brought a lot more people to the store than they had anticipated. Rebecca smiled at the thirty-year-old musher with a sizable audience crammed into the camping area.

A scream reverberated through the first floor, then another, followed by a shriek. To Rebecca's right the crowd parted, people fleeing toward the exits.

"Stick with me," Alex said in a voice of authority.

An older woman went down, several persons tried to avoid a collision but ended up running into her, falling on her. Alex pushed through the throng and offered the lady his hand, which she grasped, her eyes wide.

Someone behind Rebecca collided into

her, shoving her forward into Alex and the older woman. He shielded the lady from the impact, and they remained standing.

Rebecca noticed that the mob was thinning to the right. "Follow me," she shouted to Alex who used his body to keep anyone from running over the sixty-something lady in the midst of a stampede to the nearest doors.

When they broke free of the crush, Rebecca pointed to a place protected by a glass cabinet of knives. The gray-haired woman collapsed on a stool behind it, her eyes sliding closed as she rested her head against the barrier.

That was when Rebecca saw the gash on the side of the lady's face, blood streaming from the wound.

* * *

Alex checked on the sixty-three-year-old lady behind the knife counter to make sure she had been tended to. While the paramedics assessed Mrs. Rose, the woman he'd helped, Alex surveyed the first floor with only police and employees left. It looked like a herd of moose had trampled everything in their path, leaving behind smashed displays, products and a few other injured people.

Lying not too far away, Alex spied the reason for the pandemonium, only twenty minutes ago. Big rats. From what he could surmise there had been at least six or seven of the rodents released into the crowd.

As Rebecca evaluated the damage, she was overseeing the capture of the rats that hadn't been trampled in the rush to leave.

Alex returned to Mrs. Rose's side and asked the EMTs, "Will she be all right?"

The young man grinned at the woman. "Yes. She tells me nothing much will keep her down."

Alex handed her his business card. "If you need any help, let me know."

"Next time I need a knight in shining armor, young man, I'll call you." An impish grin graced her mouth.

Alex walked toward Rebecca, and Clint joined her. From the expressions on their faces, the flood of panicking people pouring out of the building had overflowed into the crowd watching Brian Nanuq's demonstration outside.

Why rats? Was the saboteur making some kind of statement?

Rebecca snagged his gaze, the long hours she had spent trying to make the promotion safe evident in the lines on her face and the circles around her eyes. She was a beautiful woman who looked as though she hadn't slept in the two days since the cyber and transformer attack.

Alex paused next to Rebecca. "What's happening outside?"

Clint glanced toward the exit. "Someone yelled bomb as the people rushed out of the store. Mass hysteria flew through both groups. There were four injured in the parking lot and a couple sped away so fast there was a three car crash."

"Are there enough police outside?" Alex asked, clasping Rebecca's hand next to him.

"Now that your captain has arrived, yes. I told him you were inside. Several officers are interviewing the people who stayed around. He figures this might be tied to what's been happening the past two weeks." A frown wrinkled Clint's forehead. "I was telling Rebecca before you came over that Nanuq's sled was destroyed."

"Thankfully, the crowd moved away from Kimberly. The stage was one of the few areas not bothered, so none of her things were ruined. Clint, tell Brian we'll replace any equipment damaged."

"I already did."

"Good. I had our manager escort Kimberly to the lounge. If Brian wants to join her, that's fine."

"He's already left with his dogs. The noise and chaos were upsetting them." Clint leaned forward and kissed his sister's cheek. "Don't worry about the parking lot. I'm taking care of it. I just wanted to give you a status report."

Rebecca tightened her hand around Alex's. "We need to meet after everything settles down. I already told George to be in my office in an hour. We have to get ahead of this. Were the rats the only thing that set this off, Alex?"

"From what I've discovered, most likely that's what caused the stampede inside the building. At least that's all my officers have found. Well, that and people thinking there was a bomb threat."

"After last year's serial bomber, I'm sure that's what really fueled the mass exit." As Clint left, Rebecca shifted toward Alex. "I'm glad I don't open the store on Thanksgiving like some have started to do. It's going to take us all day tomorrow to right this place. I hate asking employees to give up their holiday."

"Ask for volunteers. I will. I'm off tomorrow."

"But you always eat with your mom, sister, brother, and their families."

"If they complain, I'll ask them to come and help. That'll shut them up."

Rebecca grinned for the first time since this ordeal started. "Has anyone told you that you can be devious?"

He chuckled. "You did several times as we were growing up. C'mon. We'll take care of this together. You'll be able to open your store on Friday as expected."

"But will any customers show up after what happened today is reported to the public?"

* * *

Late Thanksgiving afternoon, Alex stood next to Rebecca at the front of the store. After a long day, Outdoor Sports and Recreation was ready to open tomorrow at six in the morning. Most of the workers who'd volunteered to help clean up had left. Clint and George were checking every exit, locking the outside doors, then leaving to spend what was left of Thanksgiving with their family.

"Thank God no one who was injured yesterday in the chaos had to stay overnight at the hospital," Rebecca murmured so soft Alex almost didn't catch what she said.

He slipped his arm around her and tugged her gently to his side. "It could have been a lot worse. When you and I have had a good night's sleep, we need to sit down and go through your customer complaints. The robbery in Fairbanks, especially during the holidays, might not be connected to what's happening here. People were injured here because of what this saboteur has been doing at this store in Anchorage. That's where we need to focus."

"A disgruntled customer, not an employee?"

"It could be either. Someone's not happy with Outdoor Sports and Recreation, but for the next couple of hours, we're not going to talk about the case. We both need a break. I have a surprise for you upstairs in your office."

She pulled away and looked him in the eye. "What are you up to?"

"Nothing. I'm hungry. I got something for dinner."

She brushed her fingertips across his cheek. "You're blushing, Alex Kincaid. I didn't know you could. You're up to something."

"It's a surprise."

"Shouldn't you be going to see your

family?"

He laughed. "Trying to get rid of me?"

"No, but I feel guilty keeping you from them today. I know it's a big deal to your mother. Isn't that why she came to the store to see you a little while ago?"

"No, she understands. Besides my sister, brother, and their families kept her occupied. There were six of my nieces and nephews running around her home. It probably looks worse than your store did yesterday."

"I still have some last minute details to take care of."

"But you need to take a break. Since you arrived, you've been working." He grabbed her hand and pulled her toward the stairs.

By the bank of elevators, she stopped. "I can't believe I'm making this suggestion, but let's use this."

"Are you sure?"

"No, not after the other day, but I'm so tired I don't think I have the energy to go up one floor, let alone three. I don't like being afraid of something. When I experienced that overpowering fear again while stuck in the elevator, it left me paralyzed at first. Since I was nine years old, I've learned to turn to the Lord. It took me a moment to tap into His strength, but once I did, I could deal with the situation."

He moved into her personal space and combed his fingers through her hair. "That's good advice. It's not always easy to put yourself in His hands totally, but we are much stronger with Him on our side."

"That's what I'm discovering. I've seen how it's changed Clint. If he could survive being a war captive and managing to escape from the enemy, then I can do this." She punched the up button on the wall.

Alex leaned in and only meant to kiss her briefly like a friend, but once his mouth covered hers, he couldn't resist her lure. He deepened the connection, pouring suppressed feelings of longing from his teenage years into it. He wrapped his arms around her and pressed her against him while leaving a trail of soft nibbles all the way to her ear.

The ding announcing the elevator had arrived penetrated his haze and jolted him from continuing what he should never have started. They were good friends. He didn't want to change that, and he certainly didn't want to be rejected by her a second time, although she never knew that.

Moving back, he swept his arm across his body and bowed. "Your carriage awaits, my lady."

She smiled. "That's okay. I'm going to let you go on first."

"I would never leave you in a lurch." He started for the elevator.

She clasped his shoulder, stopping him. Then she skirted around him and entered first. "I know, Alex. You've always been there for me." Her intense blue eyes fixed on him as though trying to delve deep into his thoughts.

Could there be more between them? He'd been concentrating on his reaction to the kiss, not hers. She hadn't pulled away. He had.

After he boarded the elevator, Rebecca pushed the button to the fourth floor then lounged against the wall, her gaze still on him. He held it, and before he knew it, they arrived at their destination. The air in the car pulsated with—needs.

But she didn't move.

And he didn't either.

Until the elevator began to close. He lifted his arm to stop the doors from shutting. "After you, Rebecca."

Then he followed her into the hallway, wondering what in the world had just transpired between them. He hurried around her and paused at the entrance into her office, facing her. "I want you to shut your eyes."

"Why?"

"I have a surprise for you."

"Remember that time in middle school when the teacher wanted us to wear a blindfold and try to navigate around the classroom. I didn't. I don't give up control easily."

"I know, but I'd like to guide you into your office." He stretched his hand toward her, suddenly her letting him lead took on a much more sufficient implication than originally considered by him.

FIVE

Rebecca covered her eyes, and Alex led her into her office. As much as she didn't like being in the dark and not in control, she trusted Alex. None of the panic she'd experienced trapped in that refrigerator surfaced, which surprised her after what happened in the elevator at the first of the week. She'd tried to put that whole incident behind her and thought she had until then.

Then the memory of his kiss earlier shoved any thoughts of the refrigerator incident from her mind. Instead, all she could think about was the feel of his mouth on her, the warmth of his touch as though he'd branded her.

Alex stopped, his arm around her. "You can open your eyes."

Her small round conference table had been set for two with a white lacy tablecloth, fine china, silver, and crystal stemware. "Is this why your mother came to see you?"

"Yes." He circled behind her desk and lifted a large insulated food container. "Believe it or not, she understood about me not coming for Thanksgiving dinner, but she knows how much I love a traditional turkey meal so she suggested this. I thought it would be nice to share with you, especially after Clint told me about your plans to stay here and work after everyone left. I'm hoping to convince you while we're eating to go home instead. Take this advice from one workaholic to another. Everyone has a limit, and this past week has stretched yours beyond it."

"But there are a few last minute arrangements for tomorrow that I need to finish."

Alex unzipped the container, filling the

room with mouth-watering aromas, and began taking out the dishes: turkey, dressing, green beans with almond slices, cranberry sauce, and pumpkin pie.

"How about doing this? Go home after we eat and come in an hour earlier in the morning. Getting some sleep will help you function better when the store opens." He finished putting the food on the table and drew a chair out for her to sit in. "I've learned that the hard way."

After she took her seat, she asked, "What happened?"

"I nearly missed a case-breaking lead because I was so tired I almost overlooked it. My captain told me to go home and come back after a good night's sleep. I did, and that's when I discovered the clue in the material I'd been going through. I started over and caught what I had missed the day before."

"I understand what you're saying, but this is my family's business. A lot of people depend on me. Tomorrow has to go off without a hitch, especially after yesterday. It's Black Friday."

"My case involved a murderer who had killed three people. Three families were expecting me to solve the crime, not to mention that the guy could kill again. And you staying tonight won't stop the person or persons sabotaging your store. You're the best person to help me come up with a list of any people who have a grudge against Outdoor Sports and Recreation. You can't do that if you're so tired you nearly fall asleep standing up."

Heat scorched her cheeks. "You saw that earlier." She'd been leaning against a counter, taking a moment to rest while deciding what to do next. Instead, she made the mistake of closing her tired eyes. She nodded off and nearly fell over, but she caught herself at the last second.

"I was clear across the room and knew I could never get to you in time. I was glad you perked up." Alex bowed his head. "Let's say grace and dig in before it gets cold."

"Thank You, Lord, for this delicious meal sitting before us, but especially for my employees and friends who volunteered to help today. I couldn't have done it without them."

"Amen," Alex said then started with the plate of sliced turkey.

Her father had always stressed how important it was for her to stand on her own two feet and not to depend on others to come to her rescue. And her dad had never understood her need to turn to God— hence he'd always been pushing her to be independent and capable of doing anything alone.

But after what had happened this week, her dad wasn't right about that. Yes, she needed to do her part, but without her friends and employees who went above and beyond their duties, she couldn't have accomplished what she had. The promo yesterday had been fun and successful until someone released six large rats and probably was responsible for yelling about a bomb, but today, a lot of helpers came in on a holiday to get the store ready for Black Friday. She never could have done that alone.

"Rebecca?"

She blinked and centered her attention on Alex holding a casserole dish with cornbread dressing. "Sorry. I was thinking about what my dad had said to me many times while training me to take over for him. I loved my father, but I'm learning what he wanted me to do isn't what I want to do." She took the dressing from Alex, releasing a long breath. "I've been trying to live up to the image he wanted, but I don't want to be that image. My marriage to Cade suffered because I was trying not to fail my father. The weekend he was killed in the hunting accident he'd begged me to go with him. I couldn't. Dad needed me to be at the new store's opening. I might have prevented Cade's death if I'd been there."

"He was mauled by a grizzly. You could have been, too."

"I'm an expert shot and could have taken the bear down before he killed Cade. He'd only wounded the animal making it even more enraged when it charged him."

"You can't blame yourself for his death. Wasn't that the third store for the company, the one your dad put you totally in charge of opening?"

"Yes. But not going with Cade that weekend wasn't the only time I'd put the business before my marriage. I should have realized if I wasn't ready to commit totally to Cade, we shouldn't have married in the first place."

"Maybe Cade should have chosen to go another weekend rather than put you in that dilemma."

She remembered the moment when the highway patrol officer had informed her of Cade's death. It had been right after she'd cut the red ribbon across the new store's main doors, and it had officially opened. Her father had hugged her and told her what a good job she'd done with the grand opening. She'd been thrilled. She'd rarely gotten a compliment from him. Then her world had fallen apart moments later. "I thought I could be a good wife and the daughter my dad wanted. When Clint entered the Marine Corps, I was the only sibling left for Dad to train to run the business. I didn't want to let him down."

Stunned that she was telling Alex

everything she'd kept locked up inside of her since her husband died, she suddenly stood, put her napkin on the table, and murmured, "Excuse me. I'll be back in a minute."

"Rebecca."

Hearing the sound of Alex pushing his chair back, she hurried into the hallway and escaped into the women's bathroom. She splashed cold water on her face, dried it off and stared at herself in the mirror. Why in the world had she told him all of that? When Clint had come back home, she hadn't even shared that with him. Every time she'd thought about that day her husband had died, she shoved it into the dark recesses of her mind.

Is that why I delve so deeply into work? So I never have time for anything else?

And why did I tell Alex? Not Clint?

The pale cast to her skin and the worried lines grooving her forehead shouted her stress. She was letting this saboteur get to her. She'd hoped for a great holiday season for the company. She wanted to use that to launch her expansion into other parts of the United States. That had been her father's dream. Then if she'd fulfilled it, she would...

What? Be happy? Content?

A knock on the door reverberated through the restroom. "Rebecca, are you all right?" Concern wrapped around each word.

She pictured Alex, and the tension gripping her lessened. "Yes." She checked herself in the mirror, pinched her cheeks to add color to them, and then headed for the exit.

The sight of Alex in the corridor sent her pulse racing. She'd known him for most of her life, but suddenly she was seeing him with different eyes. Why hadn't he married? He'd dated and even had some serious relationships. But he was still single. Was it because he was equally as dedicated to his job?

For a long moment, their gazes bonded. She didn't want to look away. The warmth in his silver-gray eyes melted the rest of her stress, as though there wasn't anyone trying to ruin her company. When he held out his hand, she took it and stepped closer.

"If you want to talk more, I'm here. It's good to let go of the past. We all have things that we hold onto, thinking we should have done them differently."

"How about you?"

"My issues revolve around my father, too, but for different reasons. All my boyhood, I looked up to him. He was my hero. That's why I wanted to be a police officer, just like him."

"And you have been. You've helped a lot of people get closure or to feel safe."

"But when my dad was killed in the line of duty, I saw what happened to a cop's family. My mother fell apart, and I became the man of the family at the age of twelve."

Was that why he'd never married? For months after his father's death, she'd only seen him at school. He'd withdrawn from her and even Clint.

She moved closer, taking his other hand and looking up into his eyes. "I know what you went through. Not then but now. When I lost my parents in the small plane crash, it rocked my world like an earthquake had suddenly shook everything around me."

"Yep. That about describes it." He tugged her even nearer until there was no space between them. He caged her against the door and delved his fingers into her hair. "You aren't the only one who's leery because of the past."

His nearness disrupted her thoughts. It was hard to focus on anything but the fact his mouth was inches from hers. She anticipated his kiss—wanted it. Her heartbeat pounded through her body. She was sure he could feel it.

She swallowed hard and tried to think about what he'd said last. She should reply, but...

His mouth swooped down and laid claim to hers. As his arms closed around her, she embraced him, pouring all her newfound feelings regarding Alex into their kiss. She hungered for it. Didn't want it to end.

But the ding of the elevator echoed vaguely in her mind.

Alex pulled away and faced the end of

the hallway, putting himself in front of her. "Are you expecting anyone?"

"No, but it could be the security guard."

Rebecca peeked around Alex as the doors opened and an older man, dressed in the gray uniform of the store's security team, exited.

Warmth suffused her face as though she and Alex were teenagers caught kissing by a parent. "Good evening, Robert. Did you have a nice Thanksgiving dinner?"

"Yes, ma'am. It's a good thing I do a lot of walking on this job. I need to after what I ate."

"I can understand that. Alex brought me Thanksgiving dinner tonight since I was going to work. Is everything quiet downstairs?"

"Yes. I can't believe you got the store ready to open after what happened yesterday."

"I didn't do it alone. People," she pointed to Alex, "like him helped me today."

Robert checked the doors. "You should have asked me. I'd have been here."

"No, I needed you alert and rested tonight. But thanks." She gave her employee a smile, then made her way toward her office and didn't breathe properly until she was inside. "That was close. I'm glad Robert isn't one of the employees who likes to gossip."

"You have a right to a life, Rebecca."

"I know. But I run a big company. It's hard to avoid the public eye, especially with what's going on right now."

"Let's finish dinner. Then you need to go home and get a good night's sleep. Tomorrow will be a long day for both of us."

"Don't you usually take the Thanksgiving weekend off?" Rebecca sat in the chair she'd vacated.

"Yes, but not this one. I'll be looking into your current and past employees as well as anybody who's been upset with Outdoor Sports and Recreation. I talked with the head of Human Resources earlier about seeing her tomorrow. I'll concentrate on people living here, but I'm not ruling out ones who've worked in your other stores."

"I'll work on it, too. Then we can compare notes."

"I think that'll be good. You'll come at it from a different perspective."

"It may take me longer. I'll still have to deal with problems that arise during the day."

"I'm going to think positive." Alex lifted his drink. "There will be no problems tomorrow."

Rebecca clicked her water glass against his. "I second that." After she took a long sip, she ate what little she had left.

Although the food was delicious, she couldn't rid her mind of the sensations Alex's kiss produced in her. She wondered what would have happened if Robert had picked another time to do his rounds. This wasn't a good time to get sidetracked with the new feelings that were developing for Alex. Or were they there the whole time just waiting for him to make a move?

SIX

Sunday evening, snow pelted his windshield as Alex drove toward Rebecca's house. He had a list of possible saboteurs he'd compiled while working with HR and doing some digging into a few employees and disgruntled customers. Nothing turned up on the security cameras, except a fleeting glimpse of a medium-built person bundled into a heavy coat and hat outside at the back of the store right before the electricity went down. He hadn't been able to discern whether the individual was a man or woman.

From what testimony the police had gathered from witnesses at the Iditarod promotion, whoever was responsible for the rats had known where to stand to avoid being caught on film. No one in the crowd knew where the warning about a bomb had come from. Even a few employees thought there had been a bomb planted and had spread the word.

At the closed gate into Rebecca's property, Alex texted her that he had arrived. Not half a minute later, he was admitted, and soon he pulled up in front of her house.

With Susie beside her, Rebecca stood in the entrance, the porch light illuminating her beautiful features. In less than a week, he'd kissed her twice. Their friendship had altered, and he didn't know if that was a good idea. He couldn't keep Rebecca at a distance like he did other women he'd dated. She knew him well, and there was too much past between them for that to work.

With the snow picking up, he jogged to her, the sight of her warming his heart as it had always done. Why hadn't he made a move on her before she'd started dating

Cade? Even some years after his father's death, he'd still been dealing with it and the added responsibility he had at home, but if he had approached her about dating, maybe things would have been different.

As he greeted her with a quick kiss on her cheek, he stuffed those thoughts away to examine another time when he wasn't so intent on finding out who had a grudge against her company.

Inside the foyer, Alex shed his coat, hat, and gloves then greeted the German shepherd. "From the look on your face, something's wrong. Is it the downturn in sales for the store for the past three days?" When he'd been there, few customers had been in the store.

"Dismal is a better word, but then I can't blame people for being leery of coming to the store after what happened last week. If I didn't own it, I wouldn't."

"How about your other seven stores?"

"They're doing as well as expected, thankfully, and online sales are steady, but the one in Anchorage usually outsells all of them put together. About all I can do is increase security and offer great sales to tempt the customers to shop there again, but I'm not going to do that until I feel they'll be safe."

"And they won't be until we catch the saboteur. Whoever it is knows your Anchorage store well. I did find out earlier the police in Fairbanks caught the robber who hit your OSR there. I told them I would let you know."

She grinned. "I'll take any good news right now. C'mon. Let's go into the kitchen. I made some sandwiches and put on a pot of coffee."

Susie went ahead of Alex and Rebecca and settled on her bed nearby. There had been a couple of times when Rebecca couldn't help with a search and rescue attempt when Alex had used her German shepherd and teamed up with Clint and his SAR dog.

Rebecca poured coffee in two mugs then brought them to the table where papers were scattered next to a laptop. "As you can see, I've been working on my list. I came home a little early today to finish. I didn't think there would be many names on it, but when I went back ten years like you said, there were more than I wished."

Alex sat in the chair next to her. "I've learned in my job, you can't please everyone no matter what good intentions you have. All you can do is the best you know how. From talking to your employees these past few days as well as your customers, you're doing that. Friday, I spoke to a man and his wife who were shopping for the holidays, and all he said were positive comments about his treatment at Outdoor Sports and Recreation. And he'd been in the store when the stink bomb went off. On top of everything, you have the best prices in town."

"I can always count on you to cheer me up. How can you be so positive with the job you have?"

Alex shuffled through his papers until he found his list then put it on top. "You must bring that out in me, but I've learned over the years that negativity only makes a bad situation worse. It's tough being a police officer, but that's the one thing my father used to tell me, and he was right. Besides, my mother looks on the negative side enough for me and the whole family."

"Our childhoods sure have shaped us." Rebecca placed her list beside his. "I put the people in order of who I think has the most motivation to ruin the company, I really didn't find any customers to add though. These are all past employees with grudges against the store."

Alex pointed to the second name on his sheet—Tom Baker. "Why didn't you put his name on yours? You fired him, and your company pressed charges against him for embezzling from the company."

"That was eight years ago. He served his time and has been out for four years."

"People can hold grudges for a long time."

"Tom has diabetes. He never took good care of himself, and in prison, he had to have part of one leg removed in the course of his time there. Gangrene spread in his foot, and by the time he reported to the infirmary, he had to have it removed from the knee down. After his release from prison, he lost the second leg." Rebecca remembered seeing Tom when he left the hospital after that surgery. She'd thought about saying something to him, but she hadn't because she hadn't wanted to bring up the past. He had enough to deal with. "Tom's confined to a wheelchair. I can't see him doing this. He doesn't have any children and his wife is dead."

"How do you know this?"

"I paid for the second surgery. He had no money. His wife came to see me and begged for help. I couldn't turn her away. I had a cousin who died from juvenile diabetes. The disease can ravish a body."

"But the wife has since died?"

"Yes, I saw that in the paper about eighteen months ago."

She amazed him—keeping up with past employees who had stolen from the company. "Okay, how about the first guy I have on the list?"

"Why did you put Neil Sanders' assistant on the list?" She tapped his third name.

"Paula Harris is knee deep into debt. She received a foreclosure on her house a few weeks ago, and she would have the access and know how to hack into your system. I vetted everyone in the Tech Support Department."

"I didn't know that she's going to lose her home. She's been working for us for several years, and Neil is thinking of promoting her. True, those factors could lead a person to desperate measures, but not Paula. You and I looked at the possible people in a different light. The guy at the top of my list is Matt Pinkston."

"Why? He's at the bottom of mine, and he's only there because he was recently fired."

"He was let go because of sexual harassment. While that doesn't necessarily translate into being a saboteur, he'd been suspected of taking inventory before things hit the fan. He was one of our stockers. I witnessed his departure and his tirade when he stormed out of the warehouse. Since then Heather Adams, the cashier he harassed, has been receiving notes from a 'secret admirer' and yesterday while I was up at the front of the store, I asked her how everything was going. I really appreciated her finding the jammer. Heather mentioned she was still dealing with Matt. She's thinking about getting a restraining order against him. Maybe you could talk to her and encourage her to follow through with that. I don't have a good feeling about the man."

Alex sipped his coffee. "No problem. I'll make it a point to see her this week. Let's go through the rest of the names. I'll take notes and follow up with a combined slate of suspects."

"First, I need to let Susie out back, and I could use some fresh air. The past few weeks I haven't been able to exercise or get outside much."

"I'll come with you, not that I'm worried with Susie protecting you. I don't want to pass up enjoying nature even though it's snowing."

"I love snow. That's probably why Alaska is so special to me. Of course, I haven't lived anywhere else but here."

"Me neither. I'm a diehard Alaskan." Alex headed for the foyer and retrieved his coat, hat, and gloves. Maybe the brisk wind and cold snow would rejuvenate his brain cells after the past few days of running down leads and investigating anyone he thought might have a reason to harm the company."

"We're supposed to get four or five inches of new snow before this is over tomorrow. Maybe you should take my notes and go home now."

"I've been in worse, and I have all the equipment I need to traverse a snow-blanketed terrain if I get stuck somewhere." Alex opened the kitchen door and let Susie go first then Rebecca. While the German shepherd bounded down the stairs and into the yard, Alex hung back with Rebecca on the deck.

She gripped the railing and leaned into it. "On second thought, I don't think I have the energy to slosh through the half a foot of snow we've had recently, but watching it fall in the glow of the security lights is calming to me."

"My favorite is the peace and quiet."

Susie barked.

Rebecca jerked straight up, looked toward her German shepherd, and chuckled. "That squirrel loves to tease Susie while sitting safely on a branch above her."

"Have you been able to relax any?"

"Not much in the past week. I do better here than other places. Susie sleeps in my bedroom with me, and I actually can get some rest then."

Alex placed his gloved hand over hers on the railing. "I can stay if that would make you feel better." Then quickly he added. "According to you once, the couch in your den is a mini bed and is probably as comfortable as mine at home."

"I hate to ask that of you and besides whoever is doing this is trying to ruin the company, not me. I very likely didn't have anything to do with what made this person go after OSR. With that in mind, I'm going to delve next into people my father angered. I love my dad, but he was never one to mince words. He was one of the bluntest persons I've ever known."

"I won't argue with you on that. I've said people can hold grudges for years, but usually you'll know about them."

"Two feuding families like the Hatfields and the McCoys?"

"Yes." Alex took another deep breath of the chilled air and continued, "Let's go tackle those names."

When Rebecca called for Susie, the dog hurried toward the deck. As Alex opened the back door for them, the sound of the phone ringing filled the quiet.

Rebecca skirted around him and rushed to answer her landline. "Hello."

Whoever spoke to her was conveying bad news because her expression immediately evolved into a deep frown, her eyebrows slashing downward, her hold on the phone tightening.

"Okay. I'll be there." Rebecca hung up and faced him. "The alarm at the store is going off."

SEVEN

While Alex made his way to the patrol officer who responded to the alarm and was now talking with the security guard, Rebecca sat in his SUV, arms crossed over her chest staring at the bullet holes that riddled the storefront's main display window. Alex hadn't wanted her to get out of the car in case the person was still around somewhere.

The snow had increased in velocity and volume. If there had been any foot or tire prints, they were covered over in the time it took for the police to arrive. She'd called Clint and George who were on their way to the store.

Alex trudged back to her and sat behind the steering wheel, a grim expression on his face. "Other than looking for the bullets used and the footage on the security camera, there's little to go by. The guard was in the second floor office, monitoring the TV feeds and saw what happened. Someone, dressed all in white, rode a snowmobile up to the window and shot at it. As Robert hurried downstairs, he called the police. He heard at least five shots, and there's evidence of five holes in the pane. All he could tell us about the snowmobile was that it was black and silver. The tape might give us more, but this happened all within a few minutes. By the time Robert reached the front, it was quiet. Once he realized no one had gotten inside, he called you. Then the patrol officer arrived soon after that."

"There are two guards on duty at night. Where's the other one?"

"He was checking the upper floors when Robert radioed him to come to the first floor. Once the police arrived, he went back upstairs to look at the security monitors in case the shooting was a distraction for something worse. I talked to him, and so far he hasn't discovered anything else."

"Clint and George are coming. I'll need to stay tonight. The store opens at nine tomorrow morning. We need to do something about the window in the meantime."

A small smile graced his mouth. "I figured you'd say that. I'll stay, too."

The idea he wanted to help her underscored she wasn't alone in this fight against an unknown opponent. "You don't have to. Clint will be here," she said to give him an out.

"I know. But this is a big building."

"Do you really think the saboteur will strike again tonight, especially since more snow is predicted?"

"No, but I'm not taking any more chances. I told you I would be here for you, and besides I'm your ride home."

She couldn't believe that in the middle of all that was going on she could manage a chuckle. "My brother can take me to my house."

"Okay, then I'm the lead detective on this case and should be here. This is much more than a prankster. A few people have been injured. I don't want to see anyone killed. I want this guy."

"So do I. Let's go inside. It's going to be a long, cold night because I'm camping out near the window." She opened the passenger door, and frigid air swept through the SUV and snatched her breath.

"Yes, ma'am. I've camped in many different environments and conditions but never inside a store."

She glanced at him and grinned. "At least we'll have some heat. It's freezing out here." She made a dash—as much as she could in eight or nine inches of snow—to the main entrance.

The thought that Alex would be here with her and the others gave her reassurance and hope a solution to the problem would be found soon. She had the income of too many employees riding on the company remaining viable.

* * *

Dressed in a rented tuxedo, Alex felt out of character Friday night as he entered the hotel where the twenty-fifth anniversary party for Outdoor Sports and Recreation's suppliers and employees was being held. Knowing Rebecca, she'd probably been here for the past hour making sure everything was set up the way she envisioned. He'd wanted to pick her up at her house and bring her—like a real date—but she hadn't been sure of her timetable.

At least since Sunday night, nothing had happened at the store. He kept thinking it was the calm before a storm. He had officers scattered around the ballroom for the evening in addition to Rebecca having added security. He prayed nothing went wrong.

The leads he'd run down had led to dead ends. The snowmobile had been stolen and was found about a mile from the store the next day. No useable latent prints were found on the vehicle. Digging into their lists hadn't produced any concrete evidence pointing to a suspect.

By the end of the week, business at the store had picked up some. Rebecca had to reassure her employees she didn't want to layoff anyone, especially at this time of year, but there were rumors flying around the staff that made this extra stressful for everyone. To cancel this celebration wouldn't have played well in the press, besides she still would have lost a lot of money due to the cancellation policies in place.

When he entered the ballroom, his gaze immediately found Rebecca across the large, festive room with Clint and his wife, Tory. Rebecca wore a gorgeous, backless, floor-length gown with long sleeves and a high neckline. Beautiful. Captivating. Enchanting.

She'd shown him the dress last night. She'd called the material gold lame. Its softness clung to her curves as he approached her. Now that he saw it on her, he realized she would stand out in a crowd as though she were a shimmering gold target.

Pulse racing, Alex stopped next to

Rebecca. "You've gone all out for this celebration. I didn't realize you could make camping gear look fancy, but you managed to glamorize it with sparkles and glitter among the gold and white streamers and balloons.

"I had fun mixing the elegant with the rugged. Tory helped me with it."

Clint's wife laughed. "Most of this is Rebecca. She knows how to throw a party."

"When do the doors open?" Alex scanned the area filled with waiters, waitresses, and security personnel.

"Any moment, which means Clint and I need to be by the entrance to greet people as they come in. He'll be at one door, and I'll be at the other."

"You didn't tell me that." Alex hated surprises.

"That's because I just thought of it. Right now my employees and suppliers need to be reassured by us personally. What better way?"

In a bullet proof cage maybe—but Alex kept that to himself. "I'll be right next to you then. Clint, I figure you can handle yourself."

"Good thing, too. See what my sister talks me into." Clint took Tory's hand. "We'll see you two later."

"A few days of calm and you're ready to parade yourself through the streets."

"Why, Alex, you sound grumpy."

"I've had many sleepless nights because of you lately. You know I was for calling off this shindig."

"Of course. But I can't let this saboteur win. Now I have bulletproof windows and doors all around the first floor of the store. Thankfully, there weren't all that many to install."

"Yes, I saw that on the news."

Rebecca frowned. "Someone leaked that to the press. I want to keep everyone as safe as possible, but when you mention bulletproof glass, that doesn't reassure some people. It makes OSR sound like a battlefield. But this saboteur is not going to win. That's another reason I went ahead with this celebration."

He couldn't change Rebecca, and he didn't want to. Her independence and determination were two things he loved about her. But in his gut, he felt they hadn't been concentrating the investigation in the right place. "The more I've scrutinized the incidents at the store, the more I think it's someone who's still working for you. An employee knows what's going on and wouldn't necessarily stand out on the tapes when we reviewed them because he was supposed to be there."

Rebecca's jaw dropped. "You're telling me this right before I'm to greet most of my employees for a night of fun and celebration?"

"I'm telling you this because I've been reviewing all the evidence, and I can't shake this conclusion. Most of the people on our lists haven't panned out."

"But why? If they aren't happy, why are they working for me?"

"I can't answer that. If I could, I'd probably be able to find them." The doors swung open. "It looks like the guests are arriving. I do feel better that the guards are screening the guests."

"Yes, only those invited will be allowed inside." Smiling, she faced the guests entering. "I haven't heard of anyone that dissatisfied to ruin the company paying their salary. We'll talk tomorrow about what you think."

He positioned himself slightly behind Rebecca and as close as he could to her. As the guests greeted Rebecca, Alex still couldn't shake the feeling the saboteur was one of the arrivals.

* * *

Rebecca scanned the ballroom full of employees, suppliers, friends, and business connections. Could Alex be right that someone who worked for her right now was behind the recent harassments that were costing her company a lot of money, as well as causing injuries to others?

Lord, thank You there are no deaths.

But what if that changed if the assailant wasn't caught soon. She knew she wasn't directly responsible if someone lost his life, but she would feel that way. Years ago, the people who worked for her were considered her family. Now with the count in the hundreds, she still felt that way toward a number of them, but so many she didn't know personally, unlike before. That was the downside of growing her business.

Alex leaned closed. "Want to dance? This will be the last song tonight."

Rebecca pushed the unpleasant thoughts away and concentrated on the man next to her who had rarely left her side all evening. The soft melody of the live music, an instrumental version of "Silent Night" pervaded the large room. "I'd like that. This is one of my favorite Christmas carols."

Alex stepped onto the dance floor and took her into his arms.

As they slowly moved through the crowd, she realized the celebration would be over when the song ended and nothing bad had happened. "I want to be by the door to say good night as my guests leave. Can we move near the main entrance by then?"

"I can't talk you out of doing that?"

"No."

"The evening has gone smoothly but—"

"That isn't the reason. When I can, I need to make a personal connection with my employees. Maybe if I'd done more of that in the past few years, we wouldn't have this problem."

He paused in the middle of the floor and stared at her. "Don't go there. What's been happening isn't your fault. And, yes, I'll move us toward the door." Then he swept her in the direction of the main entrance. "But I'll be right beside you. I won't relax until this is completely over."

A moment later, Rebecca stood near one of the exits and noticed Clint had done the same on the other side of the room. A parade of guests passed her, all voicing how much they had enjoyed the celebration and looked forward to it continuing the next day at the store.

Susan Maxwell stopped with her husband. Rebecca hugged her administrative assistant. "Thank you for all the long hours you've been putting in lately." Susan and James Collins in HR had helped with compiling all the data on the employees.

"Anything I can do to help with finding the saboteur."

"And that's why I don't want to see you until Monday. Enjoy your weekend."

After her administrative assistant moved away, Neil shook Rebecca's hand. "I wish my wife could have come, but our youngest came down with a stomach virus today. She would have really enjoyed this. I sure did."

The head of tech support was quickly followed by his assistant, Paula Harris and her husband, who Alex had discovered was an outdoorsman with an excellent reputation as a marksman. Rebecca hated her suspicions of the young woman, but she couldn't shake the reasons she was hired in the first place—her computer skills. "Thank you for coming." Forcing a smile, she shook hands with both of them and kept an eye on them as they made their way to the door.

Alex nudged her gently, and Rebecca quickly returned her attention to the guests leaving. Heat flushed her cheeks as Rebecca acknowledged the next employee and her fiancé. "Congratulations on your engagement and sharing the news with me tonight." Rebecca shook Heather's hand then Zach Walker. "I hope you two had fun this evening."

"We did, especially your toast to us. It's exciting about your expansion into the lower states."

"Only good news allowed tonight."

"Yes. I'm thrilled the store had a lot more customers today than yesterday."

"I was, too, even though it makes your job twice as hard."

"I'd rather be busy than standing around idle."

When the cashier left, Robert, on the security team and the last person nearby, approached. Not until then did Rebecca realize how tense she'd been. She managed to relax totally for the first time as she shook hands with Robert. "It's nice seeing you. I appreciate your help this past week and your quick response to the shots at the window."

"I enjoyed the evening," Robert grinned, "and not being on duty."

After Robert left, Rebecca turned to make sure there wasn't anyone left except security, hotel staff, and her brother and his wife.

With Alex still by her, she finally inhaled a deep breath and blew it out slowly. "Now I can say the evening went off without a hitch. Thank goodness. All I want to do is go home and sleep. I wish for twelve hours, but I'll have to settle for eight. Better than what I've been getting."

"I understand. I'll be at the store tomorrow, too. I know the celebration on Saturday and Sunday won't be as big as you wanted, but I think playing it low key is better. You're still celebrating twenty-five years of serving the community."

"Yes, with twenty-five percent off every item in the store. That may be more significant to our customers than anything we were planning before the saboteur hit."

"And just in time for Christmas." Alex put his arm around her waist. "I'll walk you to your car. And just so you know, I'll be following you home."

Surprise—and excitement—flitted through her. "To stay?"

He chuckled. "My intention was to make sure you get there safely although staying—as your guard—has its appeal. Until this is over with, that's where my focus has to be."

When he helped her with her coat, his hand lingered on her shoulder for a few seconds. She imagined the warmth of his palm against her skin, and flutters in her stomach were set off like a burst of fireworks.

"I'm not parked far from the entrance. That's the benefit of coming early."

At the exit, she stopped for a moment. Snow fell, the wind swirling it. When Rebecca left the hotel, she hurried in the direction of her car and clicked the button on her key for her engine to start. "The bad weather moved in earlier than expected, but it shouldn't last long—at least according to the news." At her four-wheel drive vehicle, she unlocked her door. "In case we get separated, I'm going the usual way home. I'll leave the gate open until you arrive."

Despite the brisk bite to the wind, Alex bent toward her and gave her a quick kiss. "If you have trouble. I'm not far behind you. Call if you need me." He opened her door.

She slipped behind her steering wheel, hoping the heater would warm the interior quickly. She switched it up to the highest it could go, then eased out of her parking space.

In town the traffic was thicker than she expected, even for a Friday night at midnight, but it began lessening as she drove further out of the heart of Anchorage. She saw a few car headlights behind her, comforted to know one of those vehicles was Alex's. The closer she came to her house, the more treacherous the highway became. That was to be expected with less traffic.

The lights of the city dimmed in the snowfall. When she'd been working late, there were times she'd wondered how she'd ended up at home. But she knew the route so well, she could almost drive it blindfolded. As she headed into the more isolated part of the trip, she still saw headlights behind her. She navigated her SUV around the second uphill curve with towering evergreens looming along the side of the road.

She came out of the curve and gently pressed on the accelerator. Nothing.

What in the world?

Then suddenly the steering wheel moved toward the left without her help. She attempted to wrestle the wheel and tried to brake as her car picked up speed while heading toward the drop off. Nothing.

Help, Lord.

She couldn't control her SUV as though it had a mind of its own.

Her vehicle kept going faster. She braced herself as her car flew off the ledge.

EIGHT

The light a few yards away turned green, and Alex crossed the intersection, watching as Rebecca disappeared around the curve ahead. Noting the road conditions weren't too bad, he increased his speed slightly.

Suddenly out of nowhere headlights flooded the interior and blinded him. The next second a vehicle plowed into the back passenger-side door, slamming him into the other lane and sending him into a spin until a pile of snow on the side of the road stopped him. His body was thrown forward, caught by his seatbelt then tossed against his seat. The back of his skull hit the headrest and sent him toward the steering wheel again. His head struck the hard plastic.

Horns blared. He blinked at the bright lights surrounding him.

In a wreck.

Can't be.

I have to keep up with Rebecca.

Need to call her.

With his head pounding, he fumbled for his cell phone in his pocket, but his hand fell to his side. The pain emanating through his brain demanded his attention. A dark void lingered at the edges of his consciousness.

Rebecca. He didn't want her to worry.

He touched his forehead, his fingers covered in blood when he pulled them away. He didn't have time to be injured. He tried for his phone again, but the blackness swallowed him.

* * *

A numbing cold snaked its way into Rebecca's mind and through her whole body, urging her to open her eyes. She blinked several times then forced her lids to stay open. Slowly her surroundings took shape. Faint lights from the dashboard illuminated the interior of the front. A tree branch stuck through the windshield only a foot from her took up the passenger side and the space between the bucket seats. She tried to move, but every time she did pain shot through her. Up her leg. Piercing her skull.

Where am I?

She struggled to remember what happened, but the effort fogged her brain.

She laid back against the headrest, fighting to piece the fragments of her memory together.

On my way home.

Snowing but road passable.

Alex following me.

The bank of fog threatened to swallow her. She closed her eyes and fought to recall what happened.

Everything changed. Flying through the air. Bouncing over rough terrain.

Where am I?

Unable to see out the smashed windshield, she swiveled her head toward the driver side window. A crack slashed across it, but she could look out at the white-blanketed landscape with evergreen trees, spruce, and bare quaking aspen. It appeared her car wasn't at a sharp angle or the trees wouldn't be standing so straight. She tried to picture her trip from the hotel to home and see if she could remember where she was.

A vision of her going around a curve materialized in her thoughts. Okay. Not far from her house. A couple of miles possibly.

Slowly she leaned forward and twisted around so she could glance behind her. The movement nauseated her. Before facing forward, she glimpsed the side of a cliff that stretched upward at possibly a sixty-degree angle, but she couldn't tell for sure or see the top.

How long have I been here? Where is here?

She fumbled for her cell phone in her coat pocket and pulled it free. She'd been down here for at least fifteen minutes. No bars showed on her screen. She couldn't call for help.

Did Alex see what happened? Would he be here soon?

* * *

The second the police officer gave Alex a report concerning his accident and took his statement, Alex asked the nurse in his hospital emergency room, "Where's my cell phone? It's in my coat."

"The doctor—"

"I have to call someone." The urgency in his voice must have persuaded the nurse.

She looked around her, spied something, and crossed the room. When she came back, she gave him his phone. "Dr. Stone should be getting the results of your tests soon."

"Thanks," he mumbled while speed-dialing Rebecca's landline then her cell phone.

He let it ring until her voicemail came on and left a message both places.

"Rebecca, I'm at the hospital. I had an accident. Call as soon as you get this. I want to make sure you got home all right."

The second he completed that call he made another one to Clint. "Sorry to wake you, but I'm in the ER. Someone hit me while I followed Rebecca home. I called her, and it went to voicemail. Please go to her house and check to make sure she's okay."

"If it wasn't for everything that's been happening, I'd say you're overreacting," Clint said, sleep still clinging to his voice.

"It's been an hour since we left the hotel. She would have called when I didn't arrive at her house. On top of that, there's a possibility my accident was deliberate. The truck fled the scene. The police have a BOLO out on the vehicle. The witnesses said there wasn't a license plate visible on it, but they gave the officer a good description. I have to know she's okay."

"I'm going. She'll want to come to the hospital. I'll bring her."

"Just find her." When Alex disconnected, he sat up and swung his legs over the edge of the bed.

He didn't have time to wait for the doctor and the results of his tests. He knew what was wrong. He didn't care that a stampede of moose was running loose in his head. His priority was keeping Rebecca safe. If anything happened to her...

He put his feet down and stood. Immediately, he sank to the floor.

* * *

The cold sweeping into the car through the hole the tree created in the windshield seeped into the marrow of Rebecca's bones. Her teeth chattered. Her body shook. Dressed for an evening at a gala with her short coat, not for outside in a snowstorm, she needed to retrieve the supplies she had in the rear for emergencies like this. But the tree blocked her from crawling between the bucket seats and into the back.

It wouldn't take long to freeze to death. If she didn't put on more suitable clothes, especially if she had to walk out of wherever she was, hiking wouldn't work. She glanced at the time. An hour since she went over the ledge and bounced her way down the side of the slope.

Unsnapping her safety belt, she pushed her seat back as far as it could go. Still no room for her to squeeze through and get her supplies. Then she tried to tilt the seat back, but it only went partway. Jammed? And with the headrest, she couldn't crawl into the rear.

She shoved against the door. It didn't budge. What else would go wrong?

She would have to get out of the car and find another way. But how, trapped and with her head...and leg throbbing?

Her leg? What was wrong? As she bent forward, her gaze latched onto a pool of crimson red on the floor. She lifted up her gown to reveal the piece of glass stuck in her calf, blood streaming from the wound. Not far away lay the rearview mirror, cracked into pieces. She'd known she was hurt, but adrenaline and shock must have masked the severity of her injury.

If she pulled the glass out, she'd better

be able to stem the flow of blood. Checking her surroundings only told her what she knew: her first aid kit was in the glovebox and blocked by the tree. She had another one in the back with her safety provisions she kept all the time in her vehicle, especially in winter.

She stared at the lame dress, found another jagged piece of glass on the floor, and used it to cut off the bottom of her gown. Then she took a deep breath, jerked the shard from her calf, and quickly wrapped the gash.

When she felt her head, her fingers grazed over a lump on her forehead. She didn't remember how she got it, but at least there wasn't any blood.

For that matter, how did her SUV go off the road?

A memory flashed across her mind.

She didn't have control of her car when she went over the embankment. It had sped up when she pressed on the brake. The steering wheel turned on its own. Had someone tampered with her vehicle? How was that even possible?

A cold blast of air coming through the hole in the windshield made her shiver. Even if she was warmer, she couldn't stay here. Her thoughts snapped back to what happened. What if the saboteur had caused her crash? What if he thought the best way to get back at her company was to kill her?

Or was I the target all along?

She didn't like her train of thought, but she couldn't ignore the possibility.

She had to take charge and save herself. Alex should have been here by now if he'd seen her go over the side of the highway or at the very least he should be here soon. But until she was rescued, she needed to put on warmer clothes.

She studied the driver's side window, peeked at what was preventing her from opening the door—snow—and slid her window down. A blast of frigid air took her breath away. This was her way out, she hoped.

After stuffing the items she needed from her handbag into her coat pockets, Rebecca eased herself into a kneeling position on her seat. The movement caused a white-hot streak to shoot up her leg. Her teeth gnashed together as she fought to ignore her wounds. She couldn't afford to give into the pain. She took a fortifying breath and wiggled through the opening. Once her butt cleared the window, she tumbled the rest of the way into the pile of snow that enveloped her. She gasped from the frigid air and the burning sensation of agony pulsating through her.

Quickly, she popped her head up over the rim of the hole she'd made, then struggled to stand. She prayed there was another way into her car because her feet were frozen. But when she checked the door behind the driver's seat, her hope wavered.

Keep your focus on the Lord.

She had two more doors. If none of them were accessible, then she would have to find another way into the rear of the SUV. Her last resort would be trying to remove the tree from the windshield.

When she trudged through the snow, she scanned what terrain she could make out. Her car had landed on a ledge. Only a few feet from the front of her vehicle, there was a drop off. She wasn't sure exactly how far down it was. She'd worry about that after she got the supplies she needed. Limping, she rounded the back of the car, that option was looking more and more the only solution for her. She nearly cried at the sight of a boulder up against the rear door.

* * *

Alex gripped the bed, dragged himself to a standing position, and then waited until the room stopped spinning. Carefully he made his way to his coat, shoes, and other belongings on the chair, ignoring the aches and pain of each step. As he sat and picked up his wingtips, the door opened, and the doctor entered.

"What do you think you're doing?" the older man asked.

"Leaving. I figure I have a concussion. I know what to look for. I can't stay here."

"It's a bit more than that. Your body took a severe jolt. I'm surprised you could move."

"I'm motivated. Someone I care about could be in danger." Alex finished tying his shoestrings, clutched his heavy overcoat, and slowly rose. He didn't want to let the doctor know how much the "jolt" had affected him. "See I'm fine."

"You're not kidding me. Thankfully you don't have any broken ribs, but they're bruised, probably from the seatbelt. And that isn't the worse. Your concussion isn't a mild one."

He wanted to say, "Tell me about it. Believe me, the pain is letting me know," but he needed to play it low key. "I promise you I'm not going to sleep. I'll keep myself awake, and if my symptoms worsen, I'll think about coming back here. If this wasn't important, I would stay."

Again he moved cautiously into the corridor.

The doctor followed. "You'll have to sign a form that you've chosen not to be admitted to the hospital. You should stay overnight for observation."

Alex kept walking toward the waiting

room at the entrance to the ER.

"I'll be right back." The doctor scurried away.

Alex's cell phone rang. He quickly answered it.

"Tell me it's good news, Clint." He could use that.

"She isn't at home and doesn't answer her cell phone. I didn't see her or her car along the road. She's disappeared somewhere between her house and where you had your wreck."

"That's three miles. We need to look for her. Come pick me up and bring Susie and anything else we might need, especially warm clothes and boots for me. Have Tory organize a search and rescue group. I'll report this to the police. I'll be in the hospital waiting room. Hurry."

Alex stared out the glass doors of the entrance. Snow continued to fall as he called headquarters, praying they could find Rebecca in time.

* * *

Rebecca rounded the rear of the SUV and noticed how much her car was leaning on its left side. Shivering, she hurried as fast as she could to the backseat door behind the tree. If she scooped some of the snow away from the car, she might be able to get inside.

With her gloved hands, she began digging the car out enough that she could open the door. She stopped every minute or two and stomped her feet to get her blood to circulate through them. The tingling sensation, like pins being stuck into her feet, urged her to hurry.

When she didn't think she could shovel another handful of snow away from her SUV, she yanked at the door. It gave an inch. She pulled again with what strength she had left.

Another inch wider.

I can do this.

She attacked the snow keeping her from opening it further.

Finally, she put her whole body behind shoving the door until she could squeeze inside, crawling under the tree along the floorboard. She rose behind the driver's seat and climbed into the cargo area where her emergency supplies were.

She quickly removed her unsuitable heels, slipped on two pairs of wool socks, then she tended to the gash on her leg, cleaning and bandaging it. After that, she changed into the warmer clothing before donning her hiking boots. Now she was equipped either to hike out of here or stay with the car and hope help would come soon.

Then she thought about the way her vehicle went over the cliff. Someone caused the accident and probably knew exactly where she was. She needed to get away from her car in case the saboteur came looking for her. And if she needed to leave, she might as well find her way out of here. She wished it were smarter to stay because she might be able to find out who had a grudge against her and her company.

She grabbed her backpack and put in all the supplies she might need and the gun she had in case of emergencies. It should only be a couple of miles. She'd hiked over rough terrain before but not in this much snow and not with a leg injury.

Her car was totaled so there was no reason why she shouldn't knock the rear window out with a crowbar. Thankfully the boulder only blocked the door from opening. She smashed the piece of iron against the glass until it was safe for her to crawl out. After one last glance in the cargo area for any item she might need, she made a full circle, surveying the landscape around her using her flashlight.

As she thought earlier, her car was stuck on a ledge. She carefully made her way to the edge to see how far down she would have to go. On either side of her, the shelf narrowed. To the left it ended, but to the right it continued around a corner. Maybe that was her way off the ledge and an easier path to the bottom. She only had one length of rope and didn't want to use it at the start, if possible. She sidestepped around the bend. The shelf widened. She picked up her foot to continue.

The earth beneath her crumbled, and she fell, sliding down the slope, snow tumbling after her.

NINE

Alex chose not to take any medication that would affect his performance while searching for Rebecca. A few over-the-counter pain meds were all he took while Clint drove toward Alex's wreck site. There was at least seven hours until the sky began to lighten with daybreak, but with the blanket of white on most of the landscape, seeing outside was easier than it would be in total darkness.

Alex focused on his mission rather than his throbbing head and his bruised ribs that forced him to inhale shallow breaths. *Lord, I need You. I can't do this without You.*

"We'll start where I last saw Rebecca's

car. I have some police officers looking at traffic cam videos to see if they can find anyone who might have been on that road around the time she disappeared. Then they'll conduct the interviews. Maybe they saw something or one of them could be responsible."

"Tory is organizing a search and rescue team to help. As soon as we have a location, I'll let her know." Clint stopped at the light where Alex's accident occurred. "Any news on the truck that hit you?"

"No, but the police are looking for that, too. At least the snow has stopped falling. I'm hoping if there are any kind of tracks to follow they aren't totally gone."

Clint threw a glance at the two German shepherds in the back before easing into the intersection. "At least we have Sitka and Susie. If there's a scent, they'll be able to track it and find Rebecca."

"I'm counting on that. Do you have an idea who might be after her? Maybe the person isn't tied to the company."

"My sister's whole life is the company. Most everything she does is connected to it. Her only outside activity she does is search and rescue and in that situation, she's helping people, not making them angry at her."

"How about one that didn't end well? We've had several in the past few months."

"Then why just Rebecca? She's one of many involved in a rescue mission."

Alex knew that it wasn't likely, but so far they hadn't uncovered anything about a former employee. "I mentioned to her that we need to look at current employees, too."

"That's what I've been thinking. Neil thinks the hacker did a trial run on the system a few weeks before the attack from a computer in accounting that the whole department could access."

"But not the final hack when the credit card numbers were taken?"

"No, so far the trace leads us on a wild goose chase."

"Then we should look at current employees." Alex pointed at a spot off the highway where Clint could pull off the pavement. "I saw her car before my accident right about here."

Rebecca's brother parked where indicated. "I'm letting Tory know."

"I'll get the dogs ready." Alex climbed from the passenger seat and slogged through piled up snow on the shoulder of the road toward the rear door.

He checked each dog to make sure they were dressed with shoes, coat, and other gear to protect them against the cold. The temperature hovered around ten degrees, but the wind had died down so the chill factor wasn't much lower. As Clint made his way to the back, quiet reigned with little to no traffic at nearly three in the morning. But Alex still handed Rebecca's brother an orange reflective jacket to wear over his overcoat, and Clint handed Alex a walking stick.

Alex swung the rifle he'd brought with him over his shoulder. "Let's go." Alex held Susie's leash and moved out first.

As they headed up the incline where the highway went around a curve, the drainage ditches on each side were filled with snow but not much higher. Either someone managed to kidnap Rebecca or her car went off the road. If one of those happened, there should be evidence to follow. He prayed there was some kind of clue as to what happened to her. He didn't want to lose her. Not until recently had he realized he'd always loved her beyond their friendship—probably the reason he'd never married. No one lived up to Rebecca in his mind.

God, I can't lose her now.

* * *

The breath knocked out of her, Rebecca lay unmoving at the bottom of the slope, parts of her buried in the snow that had come down with her. She was almost afraid to move. Her body ached in places she hadn't realized it could. She definitely wouldn't recommend the fast route to the bottom.

Staying with her car wasn't an option now. Good thing she'd decided moving on was probably for the best since she didn't want whoever had caused the wreck to find her. Having lived in Alaska all her life, she was used to cold weather. She knew the signs of hypothermia, and when she'd put on proper clothing in the car, it helped her, especially with two layers of wool socks and hiking boots. However, there would come a time when hypothermia would set in if she stayed outside too long.

Although animals were known to bury most of their body in snow to weather a long, cold night, the more she stayed outdoors the more vulnerable she would be to the low temperature and the person after her. She began digging herself out of the snow she was stuck in.

Freed finally, she rose, swallowing the groan, and scanned the terrain. She estimated she was probably two miles from her house. If she could make it to the highway, she might be able to flag someone down in the middle of the night even though it wasn't a busy road. Thinking about that stretch where she went over the edge, she knew she would have a tough time climbing back up to the highway. But about half a mile in the direction of her house, there was a place she could get to the road more easily.

Keeping an eye on where she was going, Rebecca headed toward the wooded area between her and her destination. Some of the evergreens looked like Christmas trees with snow heavy on their limbs. With all that had been going on concerning the store, she hadn't had a chance to put up her decorations or tree yet. She carried on her family traditions and always had the whole place done by the first week in December. But not this year.

As she put one foot in front of the other, she became angrier at how much the saboteur was affecting her life and others she cared about. One person was destroying everything she'd worked so hard for. Furious, she wanted to shout her frustration or pound her fist into the tree trunk nearby. Instead, she forgot to look where she was going, stepped into a hole, and went down. A split second later the crack of a gunshot ricocheted through the woods, the bullet striking the tree where she'd stood before falling. She scrambled behind the closest trunk. Another shot landed only inches from her, barely missing her foot, which she quickly drew up against her.

* * *

The sound of gunfire disrupted the quiet. Alex came to a halt, glancing at Clint who paused, too.

"I think it's coming from that direction," Alex said pointing northeast, off the highway. "Let's go. That doesn't bode well." He felt better with the thought of his rifle strapped across his back.

"Where? We don't know where her car is."

"It's got to be around here." Ignoring his pain, Alex increased his pace, rounding the second curve, hoping he would see her SUV parked on the side with her in it.

But there wasn't a sign of any vehicle nearby. Then shining his flashlight on the right side of the pavement, Alex spied what looked like tire tracks barely visible because of the snow but recent because they weren't obliterated.

"There, Clint." Alex trotted to where they were and peered over the slope, almost afraid to see what he thought was down in the ravine.

Clint joined Alex and they shone their lights down the incline, riddled with trees and brush. Halfway to the bottom on a large ledge, Alex glimpsed a dark shadow among the blanket of white and put on his night vision goggles to see better.

"That's her car." Alex's gaze fell on the rear roof of the SUV, one door open. Part of the vehicle was obscured by trees and shadows. "She might have gotten out." Or the gunshots he'd heard meant someone found her and killed her then hurried away. His inspection fanned outward as he looked for anyone around the vehicle.

Clint pulled out his satellite phone. "We need to get down there. I'm letting Tory know where the car is and alerting her that shots were fired."

"Does Rebecca have a gun with her?"

"She keeps one in the glove compartment and another in her emergency supplies, so it could be my sister firing. Maybe letting people who might be searching know where she is."

His gut tightened. He didn't think that was it. His wreck and her disappearance happening at the same time was too coincidental. "Let's go. Don't let me slow down you if you can go faster. As much as I wish my injuries didn't affect me, they have. I want to get to that car, but not by slipping all the way."

"Okay. When we get there, the dogs will be able to pick up Rebecca's scent if she isn't in the car."

As Alex started down the side of the bluff, he was glad Clint brought the walking stick for him. Several times his foot slid out from under him, and he steadied himself with it. *Lord, help us find her—alive.*

Rebecca's brother made it to the SUV before him. He checked it then called out, "She's gone."

When Alex approached the car, he asked, "Is her emergency equipment gone?"

"Yes, and there are two distinct sets of shoe prints. Rebecca's smaller one and the other several sizes larger. Should I send up the flare? Tory and the police should be close by now and could see the car's exact location."

"Yes. Whoever's stalking Rebecca needs to know help is close by."

As the flare streaked across the sky above them, two gunshots—one after another—reverberated through the silence.

* * *

Through the tree limbs above her, Rebecca caught sight of the flare, immediately followed by two bullets striking close by. The flare had to be someone searching for her, signaling that help was on the way. If she could hide and avoid the person with the gun, she could make it out alive. She did have her binoculars with thermal vision in her backpack. If the saboteur had the same, Rebecca needed to find a place to keep herself camouflaged with heavy foliage that gave off heat, too. She might have a chance then.

Behind her, she glimpsed a dark area.

She dug into her backpack for her binoculars and surveyed the over dense evergreens where she could hide until help arrived. Knowing Alex and her brother, this whole place would soon be crawling with people looking for her. Although she wanted this saboteur stopped now, she hoped he fled. She didn't want anyone hurt, especially her brother—and Alex. She loved him. He was always there for her, and she trusted him with her life. She didn't want to spend this life alone anymore.

Using the large tree trunk as cover, she hurried toward her hiding place as fast as the gash on her leg would allow. She dove into the vegetation, took her thermal binoculars and scanned the terrain through the thick greenery in front of her. In the distance, a heat signature of a human registered. The person lifted a gun and fired in her direction.

* * *

Alex, Clint, and the German shepherds

stood at the bottom of the slope where two sets of footprints parted.

Clint knelt by a set. "This looks like Rebecca's boot."

"Then this is the person shooting at her." Alex pointed to the prints going to the right while the other set went to the left. "So far five shots. Both are heading toward the woods. We need to go after the shooter. Once he's taken out, we can find Rebecca."

"What if she's hurt and needs help?"

"Our first priority is to take down the person with the gun. What if you approach Rebecca, and she shoots you or the gunman does?"

Clint petted Sitka and rose. "She has thermal vision binoculars in her supplies. She'll know it's one of us because of the dog with us."

"Call for a helicopter with floodlights instead. Let the police know our location and what's been transpiring. Give me a chance to get to the shooter then head out for Rebecca."

"No more than ten minutes. I'll use

cover where I can."

As Clint took out his satellite phone, Alex started out and tracked the shooter's boot prints, increasing his pace on the flatter terrain. He wished he could go to Rebecca. He needed to see she was alive, but as a police officer, he was the one who should take the suspect down. He was determined to do that. Susie wasn't trained as a guard dog, but he'd seen her once go after a wolf threatening Rebecca during a search and rescue mission.

When Alex entered the woods, he donned his thermal vision goggles and surveyed the area for the shooter. As he moved through the trees, he made out various shapes while investigating hiding places where the boot prints had led. The guy was making his way closer to the part of the forest where Rebecca must be hiding. Even if the assailant used night vision to see, they were limited to maybe thirty or forty feet. Alex hurried forward. He needed to make it to the gunman before he closed the distance between him and Rebecca.

As Alex snuck up behind the shooter crouching behind a tree, Alex signaled to Susie to stay. The figure rose and lifted his rifle.

Alex crept up to within ten feet, raised his weapon and said, "Drop your gun, or I'll shoot you." When the person didn't move, Alex readied himself to pull the trigger. "Now."

Finally, the culprit lowered his rifle.

"Put it on the ground and turn around."

When the shooter released the weapon, he leaped forward and ran.

It was almost as though the gunman knew Alex wouldn't shoot an unarmed man or he didn't care. Alex raced after him, not sure he could go very far. "Susie, find." Hopefully she would go after the assailant and his shoe prints she'd been following.

Every pounding step he took jarred him, sending pain streaking through him. But somehow his desire to have this over with and the saboteur put in jail drove him faster and further than he thought possible. Suddenly Susie came flying past him and tackled the perpetrator, stopping him until

Alex caught up.

"I've got him, Susie." While the eighty pound German shepherd hovered nearby, Alex reached down, flipped the shooter over and pulled the black ski mask off.

A wave of shock rippled through Alex as he withdrew a set of handcuffs from his overcoat.

TEN

A blaze burned in Rebecca's fireplace in her den. She sat on her couch with her legs on an ottoman, still stunned by the past night's events. She finally felt comfortable and lucky she hadn't lost any body parts due to the extreme exposure she'd suffered after the wreck. At first the doctor hadn't been sure about a couple of toes, but when she left the hospital an hour ago, he'd thought she would fully recover.

She'd heard the doorbell ring, but Martha who lived in the cabin on the property, would answer it. There was only one person she wanted to see: Alex. She glanced toward the entrance into the den and smiled.

He paused in the doorway, his eyes warm like molten silver. A slow grin spread over his features. Holding two mugs, he crossed the room and eased down next to her, only inches between them. "I brought you some hot chocolate with several marshmallows, exactly the way you love it."

She took the cup and inhaled the fragrance. "Wonderful scent." She sampled the hot chocolate then cradled it between her hands. "I thought you were going to call me before you left the police station."

"I thought you were going to rest. I didn't want to wake you up if you were."

"I can't sleep until I know what happened with Heather."

"And her fiancé, Zach. He's the one who drove the truck and ran into me to keep me from knowing where you went. He also assisted her with the rats and the day the power went off in the store."

In the woods after Alex caught her, Heather didn't say a word, so Rebecca hoped she would get some answers. "Did she ever tell you why?"

"No, but her fiancé did. We made a deal with him if he talked. I guess he wasn't that in love with Heather because he gave her up. Heather is Tom Baker's stepdaughter. When her mom was dying, she begged her daughter to continue taking care of Tom. He was bitter and blamed you for his situation, missing two limbs, losing his eyesight, needing kidney dialysis twice a week, not at himself for not taking care of himself. When he went to prison for embezzlement, he was married to Heather's mother, and his absence was extremely hard on the family. When he got out, it didn't take much to get Heather to see things from his viewpoint."

"How did she tamper with my car? I didn't have any control when it went off the ledge."

"Zach told me she hacked into your car's computer and took over driving your SUV."

For a few seconds, Rebecca relived that fear of losing control and the terror she felt as she sailed off the cliff. But God had been with her. "Why did she come to work for my company last year? To get close and find a way to hurt me?"

"She's a computer geek. Her hacking skills are topnotch. Tom encouraged her to go to work at the store. According to her fiancé, after she was hired, Tom put the idea in her head to hurt your company using her computer skills and to make your life miserable like Tom's. Whether that's true or not, I don't know."

"She's only nineteen. She had her whole life ahead of her." Rebecca lifted her drink and took a long sip. "I tried to help the family after he was released. Did you bring Tom in?"

"No. When we went to the house, Tom had slipped into a coma. He was rushed to the hospital. The doctors don't think he'll live more than a day or two."

"Hatred and revenge destroyed his life and Heather's, not mine."

Alex took her cup and set it on the coffee table, then slid his arm around her shoulders and drew her close. "Sometimes rather than to acknowledge what they did

166

wrong, they blame others in an attempt to justify their actions."

Rebecca laid her head against his chest, feeling exhausted but cherished. If it hadn't been for Alex, she could have died last night. But more than that. While she had been hiding from Heather, she'd realized life was too short to spend her whole time working. That was her father. She didn't want that for her life. Not when she came so close to dying.

God had other plans for her.

She leaned her head back and looked into Alex's beautiful eyes. "I discovered something very important. I love you, Alex. For years you've been here for me. I didn't realize how important that was until I almost lost you last night. At the celebration I announced we would expand to the lower states. I don't want to do that anymore."

"Why?"

"Because I want to spend time with you. Hopefully persuade you not to work as much and to marry me and start a family."

Alex's eyes widened then a smile that

encompassed his whole face filled her vision. He bent toward her and kissed her. "I can live with that plan. I've loved you since we were children."

She pulled back. "You never said anything to me."

"By the time I worked up my nerve, you were dating Cade. But you know, I'm not going to do what ifs. We might not have worked then. We will now." He patted his heart. "I know it in here. We realize what's important and how precious our love is."

"This will be the best Christmas ever." She wrapped her arms around him and tugged him toward her, giving him a kiss that confirmed she wanted to spend the rest of her life with him.

—The End—

Dear Reader:

Thank you for reading *Deadly Night, Silent Night*, the 8th book in my Strong Women, Extraordinary Situations Series. I love reading and writing romantic suspense stories. When I read a book, I can escape to another time and place. Reading is where I can pretend to be a duchess, a police detective or an alien living on another planet. The possibilities are limitless. I hope you enjoyed the time you spent with Rebecca and Alex in Anchorage while they tried to figure out who was the saboteur and to keep themselves alive.

Margaret

DEADLY HUNT

Book 1 in
Strong Women, Extraordinary Situations
by Margaret Daley

All bodyguard Tess Miller wants is a vacation. But when a wounded stranger stumbles into her isolated cabin in the Arizona mountains, Tess becomes his lifeline. When Shane Burkhart opens his eyes, all he can focus on is his guardian angel leaning over him. And in the days to come he will need a guardian angel while being hunted by someone who wants him dead.

DEADLY INTENT

Book 2 in
Strong Women, Extraordinary Situations
by Margaret Daley

Texas Ranger Sarah Osborn thought she would never see her high school sweetheart, Ian O'Leary, again. But fifteen years later, Ian, an ex-FBI agent, has someone targeting him, and she's assigned to the case. Can Sarah protect Ian and her heart?

DEADLY HOLIDAY

Book 3 in
Strong Women, Extraordinary Situations
by Margaret Daley

Tory Caldwell witnesses a hit-and-run, but when the dead victim disappears from the scene, police doubt a crime has been committed. Tory is threatened when she keeps insisting she saw a man killed and the only one who believes her is her neighbor, Jordan Steele. Together, can they solve the mystery of the disappearing body and stay alive?

DEADLY COUNTDOWN

Book Four in
Strong Women, Extraordinary Situations
by Margaret Daley

Allie Martin, a widow, has a secret protector who manipulates her life without anyone knowing until...

When Remy Broussard, an injured police officer, returns to Port David, Louisiana to visit before his medical leave is over, he discovers his childhood friend, Allie Martin, is being stalked. As Remy protects Allie and tries to find her stalker, they realize their feelings go beyond friendship.

When the stalker is found, they begin to explore the deeper feelings they have for each other, only to have a more sinister threat come between them. Will Allie be able to save Remy before he dies at the hand of a maniac?

DEADLY NOEL

Book Five in
Strong Women, Extraordinary Situations
by Margaret Daley

Assistant DA, Kira Davis, convicted the wrong man—Gabriel Michaels, a single dad with a young daughter. When new evidence was brought forth, his conviction was overturned, and Gabriel returned home to his ranch to put his life back together. Although Gabriel is free, the murderer of his wife is still out there and resumes killing women. In a desperate alliance, Kira and Gabriel join forces to find the true identity of the person terrorizing their town. Will they be able to forgive the past and find the killer before it's too late?

DEADLY DOSE

Book Six in
Strong Women, Extraordinary Situations
by Margaret Daley

When Jessie Michaels discovers a letter written to her by her deceased best friend, she is determined to find who murdered Mary Lou, at first thought to be a victim of a serial killer by the police. Jessie's questions lead to an attempt on her life. The last man she wanted to come to her aid was Josh Morgan, the wealthy businessman who had been instrumental in her brother going to prison. Together they uncover a drug ring that puts them both in danger. Will Jessie and Josh find the killer? Love? Or will one of them fall victim to a DEADLY DOSE?

DEADLY LEGACY

Book Seven in
Strong Women, Extraordinary Situations
by Margaret Daley

Down on her luck, single mom, Lacey St. John, believes her life has finally changed for the better when she receives an inheritance from a wealthy stranger. Her ancestral home she'd thought forever lost has been transformed into a lucrative bed and breakfast guaranteed to bring much-needed financial security. Her happiness is complete until strange happenings erode her sense of well being. When her life is threatened, she turns to neighbor, Sheriff Ryan McNeil, for help. He promises to solve the mystery of who's ruining her newfound peace of mind, but when her troubles escalate to the point that her every move leads to danger, she's unsure who to trust. Is the strong, capable neighbor she's falling for as amazing as he seems? Or could he be the man who wants her dead?

Excerpt from DEADLY HUNT
Strong Women, Extraordinary Situations
Book One

ONE

Tess Miller pivoted as something thumped against the door. An animal? With the cabin's isolation in the Arizona mountains, she couldn't take any chances. She crossed the distance to a combination-locked cabinet and quickly entered the numbers. After withdrawing the shotgun, she checked to make sure it was loaded then started toward the door to bolt it, adrenaline pumping through her veins.

Silence. Had she imagined the noise? Maybe her work was getting to her, making her paranoid. But as she crept toward the entrance, a faint scratching against the wood told her otherwise. Her senses sharpened like they would at work. Only this time, there was no client to protect. Just her own skin. Her heartbeat accelerated as she planted herself firmly. She reached toward the handle to throw the bolt.

The door crashed open before she touched the knob. She scrambled backwards and to the side at the same time steadying the weapon in her grasp. A large man tumbled into the cabin, collapsing face down at her feet. His head rolled to the side. His eyelids fluttered, then closed.

Stunned, Tess froze. She stared at the man's profile.

Who is he?

The stranger moaned. She knelt next to him to assess what was wrong. Her gaze traveled down his long length. Clotted blood matted his unruly black hair. A plaid flannel shirt, torn in a couple of places, exposed scratches and minor cuts. A rag that had been tied around his leg was soaked with blood. Laying her weapon at her side, she eased the piece of cloth down an inch and discovered a hole in his thigh, still bleeding.

He's been shot.

Is he alone? She bolted to her feet. Sidestepping his prone body, she snatched up the shotgun again and surveyed the area outside her cabin. All she saw was the sparse, lonely terrain. With little vegetation, hiding places were limited in the immediate vicinity, and she had no time to check further away. She examined the ground to see which direction he'd come from. There weren't any visible red splotches and only one set of large footprints coming from around the side of the cabin. His fall must have started his bleeding again.

Another groan pierced the early morning quiet. She returned to the man, knelt, and pressed her two fingers into the side of his neck. His pulse was rapid, thready, and his skin was cold with a slight bluish tint.

He was going into shock. Her

emergency-care training took over. She jumped to her feet, grabbed her backpack off the wooden table and found her first aid kit. After securing a knife from the shelf next to the fireplace, she hurried back to the man and moved his legs slightly so she could close the door and lock it. She yanked her sleeping bag off the bunk, spread it open, then rolled the stranger onto it. When she'd maneuvered his body face-up, she covered his torso.

For a few seconds she stared at him. He had a day's growth of beard covering his jaw. Was he running away from someone—the law? What happened to him? From his disheveled look, he'd been out in the elements all night. She patted him down for a wallet but found no identification. Her suspicion skyrocketed.

Her attention fixed again on the side of his head where blood had coagulated. The wound wasn't bleeding anymore. She would tend that injury later.

As her gaze quickly trekked toward his left leg, her mind registered his features—a strong, square jaw, a cleft in his chin, long, dark eyelashes that fanned the top of his cheeks in stark contrast to the pallor that tinged his tanned skin. Her attention focused on the blood-soaked cloth that had been used to stop the bleeding.

Tess snatched a pair of latex gloves from her first aid kit, then snapped them on and untied the cloth, removing it from his leg. There was a small bullet hole in the front part of his thigh. Was that an exit wound? She prayed it was and checked the back of his leg. She found a larger wound there, which meant the bullet had exited from the front.

Shot from behind. Was he ambushed? A shiver snaked down her spine.

At least she didn't have to deal with extracting a bullet. What she did have to cope with was bad enough. The very seclusion she'd craved this past week was her enemy now. The closest road was nearly a day's hike away.

First, stop the bleeding. Trying not to jostle him too much, she cut his left jean leg away to expose the injury more clearly.

She scanned the cabin for something to

elevate his lower limbs. A footstool. She used that to raise his legs higher than his heart. Then she put pressure on his wounds to stop the renewed flow of blood from the bullet holes. She cleansed the areas, then bandaged them. After that, she cleaned the injury on his head and covered it with a gauze pad.

When she finished, she sat back and waited to see if indeed the bleeding from the two wounds in his thigh had stopped. From where the holes were, it looked as though the bullet had passed through muscles, missing bone and major blood vessels. But from the condition the man had been in when he'd arrived, he was lucky he'd survived this long. If the bullet had hit an inch over, he would have bled out.

She looked at his face again. "What happened to you?"

Even in his unconscious, unkempt state, his features gave an impression of authority and quiet power. In her line of work, she'd learned to think the worst and question everything. Was he a victim? Was there somebody else out there who'd been injured? Who had pulled the trigger—a criminal or the law?

Then it hit her. She was this man's lifeline. If she hadn't been here in this cabin at this time, he would have surely died in these mountains. Civilization was a ten-hour hike from here. From his appearance, he'd already pushed himself beyond most men's endurance.

Lord, I need Your help. I've been responsible for people's lives before, but this is different. I'm alone up here, except for You.

Her memories of her last assignment inundated Tess. Guarding an eight-year-old girl whose rich parents had received threats had mentally exhausted her. The child had nearly been kidnapped and so frightened when Tess had gone to protect her. It had been the longest month of her life, praying every day that nothing happened to Clare. By the end Tess had hated leaving the girl whose parents were usually too busy for her. This vacation had been paramount to her.

The stranger moaned. His eyelids fluttered, and his uninjured leg moved a few inches.

"Oh, no you don't. Stay still. I just got you stabilized." She anchored his shoulders to the floor and prayed even more. Even if he were a criminal, she wouldn't let him die.

Slowly the stranger's restlessness abated. Tess exhaled a deep, steadying breath through pursed lips, examining the white bandage for any sign of red. None. She sighed again.

When she'd done all she could, she covered him completely with a blanket and then made her way to the fireplace. The last log burned in the middle of a pile of ashes. Though the days were still warm in October, the temperature would drop into the forties come evening. She'd need more fuel.

Tess crossed the few steps to the kitchen, lifted the coffeepot and poured the last of it into her mug. Her hands shook as she lifted the drink to her lips. She dealt in life and death situations in her work as a bodyguard all the time, but this was different. How often did half-dead bodies crash through her front door? Worse than that, she was all alone up here. This man's survival depended on her. She was accustomed to protecting people, not doctoring them. The coffee in her stomach mixed with a healthy dose of fear, and she swallowed the sudden nausea.

Turning back, she studied the stranger.

Maybe it was a hunting accident. If so, why didn't he have identification on him? Where were the other hunters? How did he get shot? All over again, the questions flooded her mind with a pounding intensity, her natural curiosity not appeased.

The crude cabin, with its worn, wooden floor and its walls made of rough old logs, was suddenly no longer the retreat she'd been anticipating for months. Now it was a cage, trapping her here with a man who might not live.

No, he had to. She would make sure of it—somehow.

* * *

Through a haze Shane Burkhart saw a beautiful vision bending over him with concern clouding her face. Had he died? No, he hurt too much to be dead. Every muscle in his body ached. A razor-sharp pain spread throughout him until it consumed his sanity. It emanated from his leg and vied with the pounding in his head.

He tried to swallow, but his mouth and throat felt as if a soiled rag had been stuffed down there. He tasted dirt and dust. Forcing his eyelids to remain open, he licked his dry lips and whispered, "Water."

The woman stood and moved away from him. Where was he? He remembered ... Every effort—even to think—zapped what little energy he had.

He needed to ask something. What? His mind blanked as pain drove him toward a dark void.

* * *

Tess knelt next to the stranger with the cup of water on the floor beside her, disappointed she couldn't get some answers to her myriad questions. With her muscles stiff from sitting on the hard floor for so long, she rose and stretched. She would chop some much-needed wood for a fire later, and then she'd scout the terrain near the cabin to check for signs of others. She couldn't shake the feeling there might be others—criminals—nearby who were connected to the stranger.

She bent over and grazed the back of her hand across his forehead to make sure her patient wasn't feverish, combing away a lock of black hair. Neither she nor he needed that complication in these primitive conditions. The wounds were clean. The rest was in the Lord's hands.

After slipping on a light jacket, she grabbed her binoculars and shotgun, stuffed her handgun into her waistband and went outside, relishing the cool breeze that whipped her long hair around her shoulders.

She strode toward the cliff nearby and surveyed the area, taking in the rugged landscape, the granite spirals jutting up from the tan and moss green of the valley below. The path to the cabin was visible part of the way up the mountain, and she couldn't see any evidence of hunters or hikers. Close to the bottom a grove of sycamores and oaks, their leaves shades of green, yellow and brown, obstructed her view. But again, aside from a circling falcon, there was no movement. She watched the bird swoop into the valley and snatch something from the ground. She shuddered, knowing something had just become dinner.

Her uncle, who owned the cabin, had told her he'd chopped down a tree and hauled it to the summit, so there would be wood for her. Now, all she had to do was split some of the logs, a job she usually enjoyed.

Today, she didn't want to be gone long in case something happened to the stranger. She located the medium-size tree trunk, checked on her patient to make sure he was still sleeping and set about chopping enough wood for the evening and night. The temperature could plummet in this mountainous desert terrain.

The repetitive sound of the axe striking the wood lured Tess into a hypnotic state until a yelp pierced her mind. She dropped the axe and hurried toward the cabin. Shoving the door open wide, she crossed the threshold to find the stranger trying to rise from the sleeping bag. Pain carved lines deeper into his grimacing face. His groan propelled her forward.

"Leaving so soon." Her lighthearted tone didn't reflect the anxiety she felt at his condition. "You just got here." She knelt beside him, breathing in the antiseptic scent that tangled with the musky odor of the room.

Propping his body up with his elbows, he stared at her, trying to mask the effort that little movement had cost him. "Where ... am ... I?" His speech slow, he shifted, struggling to make himself more comfortable.

"You don't remember how you got here?" Tess placed her arm behind his back to support him.

"No."

"What happened to you?"

The man sagged wearily against her. "Water."

His nearness jolted her senses, as though she were the one who had been deprived of water and overwhelmed with thirst. She glanced over her shoulder to where she'd placed the tin cup. After lowering him onto the sleeping bag, she quickly retrieved the drink and helped him take a couple of sips.

"Why do I ... hurt?" he murmured, his eyelids fluttering.

He didn't remember what happened to him. Head wounds could lead to memory loss, but was it really that? Her suspicion continued to climb. "You were shot in the leg," she said, her gaze lifting to assess his reaction.

A blank stare looked back at her. "What?" He blinked, his eyelids sliding down.

"You were shot. Who are you? What happened?"

She waited for a moment, but when he didn't reply, she realized he'd drifted off to sleep. Or maybe he was faking it. Either way, he was only prolonging the moment when he would have to face her with answers to her questions. The mantle of tension she wore when she worked a job fell over her shoulders, and all the stress she'd shed the day before when she'd arrived at the cabin late in the afternoon returned and multiplied.

Rising, she dusted off the knees of her jeans, her attention fixed on his face. Some color tinted his features now, although they still remained pale beneath his bronzed skin. Noting his even breathing, she left the cabin and walked around studying the area before returning to chop the wood. She completed her task in less than an hour with enough logs to last a few days.

With her arms full of the fuel, she kicked the ajar door open wider and reentered the one-room, rustic abode. She found the stranger awake, more alert. He hadn't moved an inch.

"It's good to see you're up." She crossed to the fireplace and stacked the wood.

"I thought I might have imagined you."

"Nope." As she swept toward him, she smiled. "Before you decide to take another nap, what is your name?"

"Shane Burkhart, and you?"

"Tess Miller."

"Water please?"

"Sure." She hurried to him with the tin cup and lifted him a few inches from the floor.

"Where am I?"

"A nine to ten hour walk from any kind of help, depending on how fast you hike. That's what I've always loved about this place, its isolation. But right now I'd trade it for a phone or a neighbor with a medical degree."

"You're all I have?"

"At the moment."

Those words came out in a whisper as the air between them thickened, cementing a bond that Tess wanted to deny, to break. But she was his lifeline. And this was different from her job as a bodyguard. Maybe because he had invaded her personal alone time—time she needed to refill her well to allow her to do her best work.

She couldn't shake that feeling that perhaps it was something else.

"What happened to you?"

His forehead wrinkled in thought, his expression shadowed. "You said I was shot?"

"Yes. How? Who shot you?"

"I don't remember." He rubbed his temple. "All I remember is ... standing on a cliff." Frustration infused each word.

Okay, this wasn't going to be easy. Usually it wasn't. If she thought of him as an innocent, then hounding him for answers would only add to his confusion, making getting those answers harder.

She rose and peered toward the fireplace. "I thought about fixing some soup for lunch." Normally she wouldn't have chosen soup, but she didn't think he'd be able to eat much else and he needed his strength. "You should try,"—she returned her gaze to him and noticed his eyes were closed—"to eat."

He didn't respond. Leaning over him, she gently shook his arm. His face twitched, but he didn't open his eyes.

Restless, she made her way outside with her shotgun and binoculars, leaving the door open in case he needed her. She scoured anyplace within a hundred yards that could be a hiding place but found nothing. Then she perched on a crop of rocks that projected out from the cliff, giving her a majestic vista of the mountain range and ravines. Autumn crept over the landscape, adding touches of yellows, oranges and reds to her view. Twice a year she visited this cabin, and this was always her favorite spot.

With her binoculars, she studied the landscape around her. Still no sight of anyone else. All the questions she had concerning Shane Burkhart—if that was his name—continued to plague her. Until she got some answers, she'd keep watch on him and the area. She'd learned in her work that she needed to plan for trouble, so if it came she'd be ready. If it didn't, that was great. Often, however, it did. And a niggling sensation along her spine told her something was definitely wrong.

Although there were hunters in the fall in these mountains, she had a strong suspicion that Shane's wound was no accident. The feeling someone shot him deliberately took hold and grew, reinforcing her plan to be extra vigilant.

* * *

Mid-afternoon, when the sun was its strongest, Tess stood on her perch and worked the kinks out of her body. Her stranger needed sleep, but she needed to check on him every hour to make sure everything was all right. After one last scan of the terrain, she headed to the door. Inside, her gaze immediately flew to Shane who lay on the floor nearby.

He stared up at her, a smile fighting its way past the pain reflected in his eyes. "I thought you'd deserted me."

"How long have you been awake?"

"Not long."

"I'll make us some soup." Although the desire to have answers was still strong, she'd forgotten to eat anything today except the energy bar she'd had before he'd arrived. But now her stomach grumbled with hunger.

He reached out for the tin cup a few feet from him. She quickly grabbed it and gave him a drink, this time placing it on the floor beside him.

"I have acetaminophen if you want some for the pain," she said as she straightened, noting the shadows in his eyes. "I imagine your leg and head are killing you."

"Don't use that word. I don't want to think about how close I came to dying. If it hadn't been for you ..."

Again that connection sprang up between them, and she wanted to deny it. She didn't want to be responsible for anyone in her personal life. She had enough of that in her professional life. Her trips to the cabin were the only time she was able to let go of the stress and tension that were so much a part of her life. She stifled a sigh. It wasn't like he'd asked to be shot. "Do you want some acetaminophen?"

"Acetaminophen? That's like throwing a glass of water on a forest fire." He cocked a grin that fell almost instantly. "But I guess I should try."

"Good."

She delved into her first aid kit and produced the bottle of painkillers. After shaking a few into her palm, she gave them to him and again helped him to sip some water. The continual close contact with him played havoc with her senses. Usually she managed to keep her distance—at least emotionally—from her clients and others, but this whole situation was forcing her out of her comfort zone and much closer to him than she was used to.

After he swallowed the pills, she stood and stepped back. "I'd better get started on that soup. It's a little harder up here to make it than at home."

"Are you from Phoenix?"

"Dallas. I come to this cabin every fall and spring, if possible." She crossed to the fireplace, squatted by the logs and began to build a fire. It would be cold once the sun set, so even if she weren't going to fix soup, she would've made a fire to keep them warm.

"Why? This isn't the Ritz."

"I like to get totally away from civilization."

"You've succeeded."

"Why were you hiking up here? Do you have a campsite nearby? Maybe someone's looking for you—someone I can search for tomorrow." Once the fire started going, she found the iron pot and slipped it on the hook that would swing over the blaze.

"No, I came alone. I like to get away from it all, too. Take photographs."

"Where's your camera?" Where's your wallet and your driver's license?

"It's all still fuzzy. I think my backpack with my satellite phone and camera went over the cliff when I fell. A ledge broke my fall."

He'd fallen from a cliff? That explanation sent all her alarms blaring. Tess filled the pot with purified water from the container she'd stocked yesterday and dumped some chicken noodle soup from a packet into it. "How did you get shot?" she asked, glancing back to make sure he was awake.

His dark eyebrows slashed downward. "I'm not sure. I think a hunter mistook me for a deer."

"A deer?" Not likely.

"I saw two hunters earlier yesterday. One minute I was standing near a cliff enjoying the gorgeous view of the sunset, the next minute..." His frown deepened. "I woke up on a ledge a few feet from the cliff I had been standing on, so I guess I fell over the edge. It was getting dark, but I could still see the blood on the rock where I must have hit my head and my leg felt on fire."

"You dragged yourself up from the ledge and somehow made it here?"

"Yes."

She whistled. "You're mighty determined."

"I have a teenage daughter at home. I'm a single dad. I had no choice." Determination glinted in his eyes, almost persuading her he was telling the truth. But what if it was all a lie? She couldn't risk believing him without proof. For all she knew, he was a criminal, and she was in danger.

"Okay, so you think a hunter mistakenly shot you. Are you sure about that? Why would he leave you to die?"

"Maybe he didn't realize what he'd done? Maybe his shot ricocheted off the rock and hit me? I don't know." He scrubbed his hand across his forehead. "What other explanation would there be?"

You're lying to me. She couldn't shake the thought.

"Someone wanted to kill you."

About the Author

USA Today Bestselling author, Margaret Daley, is multi-published with over 100 titles and 5 million books sold worldwide. She had written for Harlequin, Abingdon, Kensington, Dell, and Simon and Schuster. She has won multiple awards, including the prestigious Carol Award, Holt Medallion and Inspirational Readers' Choice Contest.

She has been married for over forty-five years and is enjoying being a grandma. When she isn't traveling, she's writing love stories, often with a suspense thread and corralling her three cats that think they rule her household. To find out more about Margaret visit her website at www.margaretdaley.com.